My Happily Ever After

Wavering emotions

My Happily Ever After

SANJAY SHARMA

Srishti
PUBLISHERS & DISTRIBUTORS

Srishti Publishers & Distributors
Registered Office: N-16, C.R. Park
New Delhi – 110 019
Corporate Office: 212A, Peacock Lane
Shahpur Jat, New Delhi – 110 049
editorial@srishtipublishers.com

First published by
Srishti Publishers & Distributors in 2019

10 9 8 7 6 5 4 3 2 1

This is a work of fiction. The characters, places, organisations and events described in this book are either a work of the author's imagination or have been used fictitiously. Any resemblance to people, living or dead, places, events, communities or organisations is purely coincidental.

Printed and bound in India

Dedicated to my late father,
Shri B.P. Sharma
(We miss you every day)

and

to all those who have fallen in love
with someone, once in their life.

Acknowledgements

I wish to express my gratitude to the people who were a part of my writing journey. I am thankful to my wife Deeksha Sharma, daughter Ritika and son Mridul for being the loving people they are, for boosting my morale throughout the journey, and also for tolerating my mood swings and giving me space to write. I am ever so thankful to my mother.

I thank all my close friends who have encouraged me with their kind words and valuable tips. Without the encouragement from my close friends, I would not have achieved the targets that I had set for myself in my writing journey. Special thanks to Dr Vibhav Sachan and Shubham Shukla for boosting my confidence with your encouraging feedback.

A big thank you to Sristhi Publishers for believing in my story and helping me bring this book to you all. I thank the entire Sristhi team for helping me fulfil my long-cherished dream. A heartfelt thank you to the editor of my book, Ms Stuti, for her insightful and flawless editing.

I thank all my relatives and English teachers who made me fall in love with the language. I thank god for being kind to me during the entire period of the creation of this book. And of course, I thank you wholeheartedly, dear readers, for picking up my book.

Prologue

This is a story of shattered dreams and redemption, of fear and fortitude and above all, of the indomitable human will. It is an inspiring story of love, romance, relationships and sacrifice which motivates the youth to live the life of their dreams.

This book is dedicated to all those who have fallen in love with someone, at least once in their life. The book is all about the journey of each and every individual's life, those who have struggled hard for getting success, and about the sacrifices behind the success.

Everyone's life starts and ends with open hands, but how successful you can become depends on you. There is no importance of sweetness without bitterness; there is no impact of love without pain.

The book tells you how important is your life and it's very easy to enjoy it. All of that depends on you, how you move forward in your life. There will be situations when you are highly frustrated and broken, but it's all a part of the journey. The book inspires people to fight their inhibitions and overcome them and lead a good life to achieve their dreams, passions or calling.

The story revolves around a young boy Keshav and his friend Aditi. Keshav is a small town guy from a conservative family in Gorakhpur. He is passionate about reading and writing since childhood and wants to make it big in the world of writing, by becoming a world famous author. But, his parents want him to be an engineer. So, driven by his parents' dream and expectations, he works hard, gets selected and takes admission in a leading engineering college in Delhi to pursue B.Tech. Since he hails from a small town, the big metropolitan city is intimidating for him and he struggles to fit in. He adjusts himself in Delhi. An idealist, studies are his first priority. He is a brilliant student and stands first in the maiden year of the course. However, in the second year, he gets attracted to a beautiful girl in his college. He is shy and studious, and falls in love with Aditi, who is completely opposite to him. She is a cheerful girl from Delhi, and like Keshav, also does not want to be an engineer. She sings sings well and dreams of becoming a great singer some day. She teaches Keshav to value himself, to live the life of his dreams and to love himself. The two soon develop chemistry and become best friends. It is obvious that they are destined for each other. As they grow closer, fate intervenes and tragedy strikes.

As a result of non-stop upheavals in his life, Keshav suffers from stress, depression, anxiety, distrust and disbelief. The story depicts his struggles, determination, and his faith in himself. The book also describes the struggle of Aditi, her firm determination and faith to achieve her dreams and the love of her life.

True love never dies. It is redefined every time you feel it. When Keshav falls in love, little does he know the impact it is going to have on his life.

1

I, me and myself

30 May 2011

I woke up suddenly, with a jerk. "What's the time now?" I murmured and looked at the wall clock: it was 4 a.m. I pulled myself out of my bed, went to the kitchen and had a glass of water before moving back to my room. I sat on the bed and was staring outside the window; the surroundings were still in the lap of darkness. I stumbled out into the balcony, still yawning. As I was not used to waking up so early, I was a little frustrated. But, as I looked around, the frustration and unsettlement were replaced with an undefined satisfaction. There was a wide emptiness and silence in the surroundings that I liked the most. The wind was blowing gently and was rushing towards me from every direction. Soon, I started enjoying the cool breeze.

Before I go any further, let me introduce myself – I am Keshav Dixit, an eighteen-year-old guy. As everyone is quite tall in my family, so am I. I live in Gorakhpur, U.P. and belong to a middle class family. My father is a teacher in a government college in Gorakhpur, so he has a limited income, and my mother is a homemaker. I have a younger sister, Garima. And being a boy in a traditional family, I was the lifeline for my parents. My parents had really worked hard in my upbringing. Making me study in DAV, the English medium school in the town, was their biggest achievement. They wanted to give me the best of schooling. My studies and career have been the top priority for my parents. Because of the great schooling, teaching and individual learning, along with the religious atmosphere in my home, I have been an outstanding student, securing more than 95% marks in both 10th and 12th standards. The teachers liked me, maybe because I was very obedient and studious. I would even help my classmates with their doubts. My mother used to give me a big lunch box with lemon rice, curd, vegetables, fruits and snacks, as she felt I needed so much because I studied hard. My parents used to take me and my sister out to restaurants, once a month. I would invariably order *masala dosa* or *poori masala* or *pao-bhaji* and would never grow tired of it.

I was an emotional and shy guy. I thought my mother was my ultimate moral compass in life. My whole existence was wrapped around making her proud and never letting her down. Since childhood, I have been encouraged by my parents to become an engineer, from one of the IITs. However, my dream was to become a world famous author. I was fond of reading and writing. Mom would always say that writing was in my genes. I salute my primary teachers for instilling the habit of reading and writing in me. I don't know precisely what inspired me to read and write, maybe all those comics that I had read during my summer vacations or those thick books that transported me to imaginary worlds and fuelled my imagination over the years. While reading or writing something interesting, I usually would lose myself with no count of time. I had also won various writing and essay competitions, both inter and intra school. I have always dreamt of pursuing my passion as my profession.

However, my parents were adamant and thought differently. I tried to convince them several times, but in vain. When asked about becoming an author, my dad would tell me that writing books could not provide bread and butter for life. He was firm in his decision, "My son will be an engineer." But, I could never understand what engineering was. So, to fulfill my parents' dream, I joined a one-year course in a reputed IIT-JEE engineering coaching: Vidyamandir Classes. Lord Narayana (Lord Vishnu) is both my best friend and my favourite. I always prayed to him before going to school. There was a Laxmi-Narayana temple near our house. I would make it a point to go there twice a week and offer prayers. This gave me immense peace of mind. On special occasions, I would go with my parents and would stay through *abhishekam* and *aarti*.

During my preparatory days for engineering entrance exams, my only job was to eat and study. My life revolved around physics, chemistry and maths. My IIT-JEE entrance exams were around the corner, and I really needed to focus. I was busy revising everything and attending mock tests every day to judge my preparations.

It was mid-May and my entrance exams were over. I felt like a free bird.

Everything looked beautiful and fresh. Lying buried in my bed during my vacations, I used to daydream about getting into my dream engineering college.

I was getting jitters as the result was to be announced today. Perhaps, that was the reason I woke up at 4 a.m.

My room was poorly furnished – a table and a chair, an old trunk on which a TV set was placed, a door connecting my room with the other parts of the house and my bed. Further, all the light and air in the room came in from the lone window in the room, covered with a thin and old curtain. The walls of the room complimented the dullness of the décor, mostly with a number of posters and calendars. I walked back into my room and tried to sleep again.

It was seven in the morning when I heard my father talking on the phone, "Oh, let me wake him up!" he said and rushed towards my room.

I was trying to figure out what was going on when Papa knocked on my door.

"Beta, get up, your IIT-JEE entrance results are out on the internet! Come fast with your roll number to the dining room. I am getting the laptop."

My eyes opened wide in shock. I was turning pale and my ears buzzed, so I couldn't hear anything else. My heart was beating as fast as a train; I could feel the strain on my head. I jumped out from my bed and pulled out my enrollment letter.

I rushed to the dining hall and saw Papa, Mom and my sister waiting for me. After seeing their faces, I understood they were more anxious than me. My mother was praying, which was apparent from her face.

My heart started pounding heavily; my mind started hovering, anxious to know the results. My eyes were fixed on my father, waiting to hear the results, my hands clenched into a fist now.

"Keshav, my son! You have cleared IIT-JEE entrance exam with a score of two hundred and seventeen and rank 4723," he said coolly.

Listening to this, I was unmistakably baffled, because I had expected a lot more than that. Instead, I began to ponder about how I could have gotten such low marks and rank. I had done my real best in the subjects. I didn't have an answer for this doubt.

Mom said, "Less than we expected." Her face was no longer illuminated.

"Your score and rank are fine, but you have scored less in chemistry. I don't think you will get any IIT with this rank," Papa said.

I nodded in agreement.

My mother and Garima were standing beside me. Mom had expected my rank to be suitable for some IIT. A long discussion was held between the four of us and finally, it was decided that I would attend counseling of all premier engineering colleges in Delhi NCR if invited including IITs. My father was slightly worried about sending me so far. Nevertheless, he was determined to send me to Delhi. After this decision, I saw a glimpse of happiness in my mom's eyes. She screamed in joy, "Finally, my son will become an engineer." Even though it was something I never wanted, I was happy to see my mom happy. I was going to be an engineer after all.

After having breakfast, I came back into my room. To kill some time, I was watching *Ramayana* with deep concentration, when someone's anxious yell broke the silence. It was my mom.

"What's it mom?" I said carelessly, without moving my eyes off the television screen.

She yelled back that Mayank had been calling out for me for the last five minutes. I rushed out of the room.

The sun was on its way to start a new day.

"Keshav, where are you bro? I have been shouting for the last fifteen minutes!" He sounded annoyed and disturbed.

"Okay, it's so early in the morning. What's the matter?" I asked.

"Will you please come down?" he said, now in a softer tone, though his eyes still had that glint of frustration.

He was in a white T-shirt and blue trousers. His dishevelled hair and dress indicated that he had come straight from his bedroom.

"The results of IIT-JEE entrance exam have been declared," he broke out.

"Oh, yes, I know. I have already checked on the internet," I said.

"Oh, really?" He was surprised to know.

"I scored two hundred and seventeen and rank 4723," I said again.

"That's really great," he said.

"What about you?" I enquired.

"I also cleared, but got 10234 rank," he said in a sad tone.

I knew he too wasn't happy with this result.

"What about the others?" I asked again.

He said, "Not so great. Priyank got 15391 and Manav got 18762."

I was really surprised now, as they too were expecting better score and rank, just like me.

"Come on, let's us have a discussion of admissions in engineering colleges," he continued.

"Yes, of course," I said. "Meet you in half an hour at your home."

He left, agreeing.

Mayank was one of my oldest friends since I joined DAV school. We played together and were very good friends.

I went to Mayank's house after some time; Priyank and Manav were already there. We discussed extensively about the results and explored the possibility of admission in IITs or some other premier engineering colleges. However, every one of us was unhappy with our respective results.

I made up my mind that I would work hard to become an engineer. It was still an honorable post to have in the world.

After much ado, my parents and I decided to close on DTU Delhi for B. Tech in ECE. I started preparing for hostel and packed my essentials.

"Have you packed everything?" Mom asked.

I knew she was suppressing her tears. Mothers are like that. But all that said and done, my mother is the biggest blessing in my life.

"Yes," I replied.

She tried to conceal her desperation. I always sensed it when she tried to hide her feelings. As soon as I looked at my mom and saw tears in her eyes, she retraced her steps to her bedroom.

The purest love in the universe is the love of a mother, and no love in the world is greater than a mother's love. Mother is the only person who works around the year without any leave.

It was very painful for my mother to see me leaving her. Anyway, I was ready for a new chapter in my life.

2

My Dream Life Begins

Reaching DTU, Delhi
16 July 2011

On the scheduled date, we left Gorakhpur. I bid farewell to Mayank, Priyank and Manav, who were also going to their respective colleges, away from our native place. We all promised to keep in touch and I was sure I was going to miss them; after all, we had been together for most of our childhood.

It was a long journey to Delhi, spanning almost an entire night. We reached New Delhi railway station the next morning. DTU, Bawana Road Campus was around one-and-a-half hours away from the station.

After completing the counseling and admission process, we went to the hostel allotted to me inside the campus. The name of the hostel was Aryabhata.

When we settled into my hostel room, my father started giving instructions to me, "Keshav, my son, you have to study hard, like you have studied in your school life. You are at a very crucial juncture of life. You have to handle everything by yourself from now onwards. I have worked hard to keep you happy and to satisfy your every need. We have a lot of expectations from you and I know you will never disappoint us. Be a proud engineer in the family and be careful with the money, always."

His words were cemented in my heart and soul.

"Okay Papa," I nodded. "I will follow all of your instructions," I convinced him.

"Have you kept the money in a safe place?" Mom asked, standing outside of my hostel, waiting for a taxi. My parents were ready to leave by the evening train.

I nodded, trying hard not to become emotional. I got a grip over myself to avoid my parents, especially my mother, from breaking into tears too. I touched their feet for their blessings. They kept advising me about various things, though soon a taxi arrived and my parents left me for a new life in Delhi.

In fact, it was a bigger heartbreak for my mom to send her son to a faraway place. But, somehow she seemed prepared, as dad had been telling her that I would be moving out to achieve heights in my life.

Engulfed in such thoughts, I reached my hostel room. It was on the second floor. I looked around it carefully for the first time. To me, it looked charming and better than my expectations. It was even better than my own room back at home.

First day of college

18 July 2011

I was expected to reach college by 9:30 a.m. on the first day. On my way to college, I thought about how my parents' dream had come true. It was their dream that I study in a premier engineering college. I entered the class excitedly. The college campus was as good as I had expected. The entrance was impressive. The classroom resembled a movie theatre with each row more elevated than the one below it. I sat in the last row from where each student in the classroom could be seen clearly. It was a huge classroom allocated to first year ECE students.

At around 9:20 a.m., few girls entered the classroom in small groups.

Suddenly my thought process was interrupted.

"Good morning, sir," every student in the class screamed in unison.

"Good morning, my dear students," the professor replied.

A heavily-built professor with a pot belly and white hair entered the classroom. He was Professor Murty.

First, he started to take attendance by calling out the name of each student. Contrary to his physique, Murty sir's voice was very thin and soft. The first lecture was quite interesting. I sincerely listened to what the professor was saying. After the lecture was over, there was a workshop.

After the lunch break, Professor Rajeev Tyagi, our engineering graphics teacher, entered the class. He taught us half cut diagram and we were made to draw its plan and elevation. All the students were struggling and glancing at each other's desk for help. I finished the task first and started explaining stuff to all the other students.

I started talking to a guy sitting beside me. His name was Vivaan. He was an average looking guy, almost of the same height as me and hailed from Lucknow – my own region. He seemed very friendly. He also stayed in the same hostel as me.

We had lab periods in the second half. Laboratory classes in engineering are always an opportunity for students to spend time together. The boys could flirt with the girls during that time.

In a few days, I had made friends with Vivaan, Chirag and Reyansh. Coincidently, they belonged to my native region, Uttar Pradesh, and we stayed in the same hostel. I had a good time with them during the first few days in college.

After joining DTU, I simply fell in love with the campus – the library, the professors, the company, mixed bunch of classmates. It was indeed a dream came true. There were so many things to learn, as it was a big leap from school. I started enjoying every moment of it. I had lots and lots of things to share with dad and mom every day over phone and they were happy for me. I used to send so many pictures of my college life to my parents on WhatsApp.

As time passed, I adjusted myself in college and hostel life and tried to suppress my life passion, i.e. reading and writing.

Life in big cities is not so easy, especially in Delhi, where the weather also does not support you. Extreme hot in summers, extreme cold in winters, roadblocks, traffic jams, water pouring in the rainy season, and dense fog lasting for months, especially in January. Life in Delhi is very fast. Wherever you go for work, you will find people standing in a queue. Even want to eat a burger or a pizza? You have to join the queue first, everywhere.

So, time started to pass at its own pace!

Life had really changed for me after coming to Delhi. A sudden change of environment had sidelined my passion to become an author. However, I continued to study hard.

I was totally absorbed in my studies. I became a bookworm, unaware of my surroundings. I would spend some time with my friends Vivaan, Reyansh and Chirag. They were such a lively lot, chatting, playing and pulling each other's leg. Extroverts make themselves comfortable as they are more confident and draw others, while introverts like me gain confidence only when they are accepted.

Life was fun in DTU. You got to be whatever you wanted to. From artists, musicians, singers, orators, dancers, writers, programmers, athletes… you'll find every damn talent over here. If you're in DTU, you can never get bored. Every now and then, you'll see a fest coming your way.

3

Engifest

One of the most awaited cultural events in DTU, Delhi was the Engifest. The night events are simply amazing. The three days of the Engifest are the most awaited. It's the time which makes you enjoy your life. Engifest aside, we still get a long chain of events.

There are some good food spots inside the college itself. There are ample places in the college to chill. You can stroll in the campus forever and still not be tired. Also, there are some famous photo session spots.

Though I managed to strike up conversations with some of the gi ls in my class, I could never think of one as a girlfriend.

I would often wonder if I would ever fall in love as I believed that it would add so much spice to one's life. I envied my friends and classmates when I saw them getting along with their girls. My mind was occupied with my studies and career. I used to console myself that I would definitely find love, but a little later in life, and when it would happen, I should be in a position to shower that special person with all my love.

First semester exam

Days passed by quite uneventfully. It was around late November, 2011 that our lectures and practical classes got over. We were given a preparatory leave for ten days as our first semester exams were around the corner. Everyone was working hard to get good marks.

The day of the exam arrived, undoubtedly the most atrocious day in anybody's college life.

All my papers went very well due to my hard work and it was a pleasant experience for me. Winters in Delhi are extremely cold. After the first semester exams were over, I went back home for ten days during the semester break.

The days at home were quite enchanting. Mom, dad and Garima were happy as never before. The pride in having a DTUian son back home meant something big for them. Meanwhile, numerous juniors and DTU aspirants flooded my home to know my experience of DTU life. I happily attended all of them and answered their curiosity.

Second semester and missing 'someone special' in life

I was in the second semester. I wasn't a fresher any longer and it was time to open up and get involved in the activities around me – celebration, enjoying, talking freely to people around me.

In the first enjoyment, I had been rather quiet and not many people knew much about me.

"First semester results are out on the internet." The news spread through all the rooms of the hostel.

We heard groans of pain and the joy of satisfaction at the same time, coming from different rooms.

I secured 87%marks and topped ECE first year. I was jubilant. Everybody was congratulating me. I immediately conveyed the result to my parents in Gorakhpur. They were extremely happy. "My son would definitely get a government job now if he continues like this," said my dad.

After the declaration of result, I earned huge respect from my faculty, and fame in DTU, making me highly confident for further studies.

So, time ran through at its own pace. No major events happened in the second semester. I studied hard as usual and also started writing a book, covering an inspirational fiction story. However, sometimes, I used to feel low. I didn't know why.

Frustrated, one day, I poured down all my feelings in my diary…

"Why am I feeling low?" I asked myself, "What am I missing in my college life here in DTU?"

I thought and said to myself, "I am low because I want someone in my life like other guys in college. I desperately need someone to share my thoughts, feelings and emotions with. I am frustrated because of the monotony in my life. On one side, there is an insurmountable academic load, and on the other side, there is loneliness in my life. My personal life is totally dark, with no light coming from anywhere."

"Oh almighty Lord Narayana, please give some light here. I just need someone to hug me and tell me I'm not as worthless as I think I am," I prayed to god.

The emotional outburst in my diary made me sad. I broke down and cried. After some time, I observed an unusual serenity in my heart. I began feeling light and optimistic.

When I went home during the summer break after the second semester exams, I started to spend some quality time with my family. Sometimes, I used to go for outings with my school friends Mayank, Priyank and Manav. However, at times, I would feel low and sad, probably due to the lack of a girlfriend. Meanwhile in June, the results of the second semester were declared. My hard work paid off once more, and I secured first position. My parents were proud of me.

4

Finding 'someone special'

28 July 2012

I was returning to Delhi for my second year. However, I was one week late for my second year classes due to the sudden illness of my mom, so I preferred to stay with her.

I was supposed to reach the college around 3 p.m. but I overslept in the afternoon and got late.

The sun was shining brightly when I saw the time in my new watch, that my father had gifted to me. Damn! It was 4 p.m.! I rushed to the bathroom. I didn't want to be late. After all, it was my first day in the second year. I put on my favourite white shirt and blue jeans, and hurried to the college. Finally, when I reached, I found that there was a cultural function going on for the freshers. Hoping that I was not too late, I struggled to reach the auditorium.

Soon, I entered the auditorium, filled with a large number of students, faculty and college staff of DTU.

Thank god! It wasn't too late.

I took a seat beside my friends Vivaan, Reyansh and Chirag and noticed that a lot of first year students were there with their parents.

Dr Shekhar, our Dean of Students' Welfare entered the auditorium. He was tall, with his pot belly almost covering his lower abdomen. I was least bothered about his speech and more interested in the cultural events.

The 'informative', tedious speech finally ended. What a relief!

After some more usual speeches, the cultural programs started. Second year students from various branches started to present their events.

I was enjoying the evening. I also enquired about the class proceedings from my friends, which I had missed, being ten days late.

The last event of the function was a solo song by a girl.

A tall girl appeared on stage with her guitar.

As soon as I looked at the girl on stage, I was smitten-at-first-sight. She was damn beautiful! I had never seen such an innocent beauty in my life. For a person from Gorakhpur and that too for a bookworm like me, it was a pleasant sight.

She wore no make-up, yet her beauty was touching the pinnacle of charm. Long silky lustrous hair, glistening snow-white teeth fabricating an impeccable laughter and radiant glow on her face left me spellbound. She wore black fitted shorts and a sleeveless sports vest. Her height was almost equal to mine. My eyes were wide open, adoring her every aspect, when suddenly she started to introduce her, "I am Aditi from second year ECE and I will present a song for you."

I was baffled to hear this. "How can she be in ECE? I have not seen her in the entire first year in our ECE department." I looked at Vivaan. He was smart enough to understand my intention. He clarified, "Actually, she is right, she is in ECE second year. She has changed her branch. In first year, she was in CSE and now she is in ECE. Since you have come late so, you are not aware."

Meanwhile, Aditi held the microphone. Music started to play in the background and everyone was stunned the moment Aditi started to sing. "She is so good at singing," Vivaan said.

I was surprised and angry at the same time when I noticed that every guy in the auditorium was looking at Aditi with the same appreciation as I was. I was possessive about her; it was the first time in my entire life that I felt like that.

As she completed her song, the auditorium applauded for her and she got a standing ovation from the entire crowd. She was one of the most beautiful girls I had seen till that day. I couldn't take my eyes off her. I forgot I had to return to the hostel. I only wanted to talk to her. Maybe I could tell her she sung very well. But I was not sure how to approach her.

I was lost in my thoughts when suddenly she turned her glance on me. I couldn't take my eyes off her. She caught me staring at her. I could not move, as if I was a statue. My eyes were glued to her eyes for quite some time when finally she felt abashed and I realized that I had stared at her for too long. She turned her glance away. I turned around quickly to find my friends. Everybody else present in the auditorium had gathered around her to congratulate her and I didn't want to be just another face in the crowd. So, I decided to walk away without anybody noticing me.

Back in the hostel, I could not get myself to sleep. I was longing for Aditi, so much that it even astonished me. I lay in bed, constantly thinking about her.

5

And so it began

Next day, I went to attend my first class for the third semester. I saw Aditi already sitting in the first row with other girls. I deliberately sat diagonally across to Aditi. She looked elegant with her spectacles complementing her beauty. My heart was in my mouth and I was spellbound.

During the lecture, too, I was looking at her. She was too irresistible to take my eyes off her. Too beautiful!! My friends noticed it and began teasing me.

Oh god! She must be thinking of me as a psycho as she had noticed that I was ogling at her.

In the second half, during our lab period, Mohan Srivastava sir gave some difficult circuits to design. Except me, every other student was facing difficulty. To prove myself a genius in front of Aditi, I started explaining stuff to other students. I tried thrice to reach out to Aditi, but she looked busy with her assignment. She didn't look at me even once.

After an hour of continuous efforts, I realized that I didn't have the courage to talk to her and started focusing on my circuit designing. I completed the circuit assignment in specified time. After the lab, the last lecture was of Digital Electronics. Murty sir while taking the attendance, called my name, "Keshav Dixit".

I politely replied, "Present sir."

He paused for a minute and said, "Dear students, Keshav, the first year DTU topper, a brilliant student, is back. I have always admired him and I urge you all to welcome him with a huge round of applause."

Suddenly, the whole class started applauding me. I felt highly honoured and equally amused. Aditi too was looking at me with praise in her eyes. I felt highly elated.

"Hey," a perky voice startled me. I had been scanning the department main notice board in the corridor after the last lecture.

I turned around. I had been praying for this to happen for the last twenty-four hours.

"Aditi?" I said.

She smiled, "You remember, right?"

Did I remember? I wanted to tell her I had not forgotten her even for one moment since her performance yesterday.

"Of course," I said. "Nice to see you."

"I wasn't sure, actually," she said and pointed to the notice board. "Is that the revised time table of second-year ECE?"

I nodded. She smiled at me again.

The notice board also had a bunch of stapled sheets with the names of all second year ECE students with their new roll numbers.

"What about you?" I asked while she looked at the notice board.

"I was in CSE in the first year. Now, after branch change, I am in ECE. I am Aditi; Aditi Kohli," she replied.

I was very happy to talk to her.

While I was mesmerized by her, she received a phone call.

"Hi, Mom," she said. "Yes, all good. Just finished today's classes… will reach home within an hour."

Her sweet voice was music to my ears. She was looking so beautiful that I couldn't measure it at that moment. Her way of talking, her friendly manner, the movement of her shiny eyes, the parting of her fluffy lips, gestures of her hands. I liked how cutely she talked, her hands moving about animatedly. All these things made me nervous.

She spoke for another minute and hung up to find me looking at her.

"Moms, you know," she said.

"Okay," I said.

We walked down the corridor towards the main gate of the college. So, I had her with me for five more minutes.

"You belong to…?" she again asked.

"Myself from Gorakhpur, UP," I said quickly. "And you?" I asked.

"From Delhi Itself," she said. "You have made friends here during first year class or in hostel?" she asked.

"Not many, only few," I said. "And you?"

"I have some classmates here from schools. In addition, I am from Delhi, so I have many friends outside as well," she replied.

"I am still taking time to adjust here in Delhi," I said. "Sometime, I feel I don't belong here."

"No, it's not like that. You will soon become a part of Delhi," she said. "Which residence have you got this time?"

"Ramanujam hostel," I said. "How about you?"

"They don't give hostel to Delhiites. I'm a day scholar," she said.

We reached the main gate and Aditi turned towards the parking lot, where her driver was waiting with silky silver Innova.

"Bye, Keshav," she called back.

"Bye," I replied.

I wanted to continue talking to her. However, I could not gather the courage. Being an introvert, I had always lacked the instinct to impress girls. She walked away and I longed to talk to her again. This particular moment was going to reside with me forever. It was like that moment which became the turning point in someone's life. I was in heaven, with all those guitars playing a sweet symphony all around me. I wanted to dance in the garden.

After meeting her for the first time, I was captivated by her. She had a pretty face and a most lovely smile. Her twinkling eyes had the cover of spectacles and lips had a pink hue. She had a grace of her own and walked as if she was the princess of a faraway land. I felt deeply infatuated toward her.

So, from my first day of second year in college, I had a crush on Aditi Kohli, second year ECE student, my classmate, the most beautiful girl on the planet for me.

I came back to the hostel, full of joy. After taking dinner, I came back to my room and lay in bed, constantly thinking of Aditi. Suddenly, something popped on my mobile screen, and unbelievably, it was a friend request on Facebook from Aditi. I couldn't control myself and immediately accepted it. She went offline. I searched her on Facebook and other social media as well. Her picture finally appeared. I liked her profile picture carrying a guitar in her hand with the caption: *Music is my life*.

I tried to sleep after that, which was actually a bad idea. For me, sleep that night was like the baby who ran away from her mother. Every time I tried to sleep, I ended up thinking of her, thinking of what could happen next between us.

I was sitting in my hostel room when Vivan, Chirag and Reyansh came to my room.

"What happened? Why are you blushing?" Vivaan asked.

"Nothing," I replied.

"Tell us, what happened?" Reyansh insisted.

"I spoke to Aditi," I told them.

"Seriously? Great, bro!" Vivaan was amazed.

"What did you talk about?" Chirag asked.

And I told them the whole conversation. They started teasing me, "Now, Keshav also has a girlfriend!"

This was how my friends got to know about my friendship with Aditi. That was what I called it, but I was not sure if she really considered me her friend, yet. Still a long way to go!

6

We had to be friends!

I woke up early the next morning, at around seven, and left for college. I reached at 9:15 a.m. sharp. Aditi was not yet in class. I took a seat at the back, as usual.

The lecture started at 9:30 a.m. and I was eagerly waiting for Aditi to come to the class. After five minutes, Aditi came in. I looked at her and my heart again skipped a beat. She sat in the third row. Once settled, she turned to look behind her. Our eyes met for a fleeting second and I felt like our souls had united.

I thought I was physically attracted towards her. I told myself it was purely lust and nothing else. Love couldn't happen in a second. But it wasn't just lust either. I was thoroughly confused. I still couldn't get her out of my mind. I wanted more of her attention. My attitude and my dressing style changed too.

I just wanted to get closer to her, but was hesitant, being an introvert. I knew that she liked me too, due to my reputation of being the first year topper. But still, I was reluctant.

Meanwhile, through Aditi's close friend Nidhi, I came to know that Aditi had been very upset with the attention she was getting in B. Tech first year. She was so beautiful and tall that almost every boy had a crush on her. Many of her classmates and even seniors had proposed to her, but she outrightly rejected every proposal.

She just wanted a true friend, but the boys wanted undue benefits from her.

A few days later, we had Signals and Systems Computer simulation lab. I picked the computer in one corner. Reyansh was sitting beside me. Aditi entered the lab. The professor explained and demonstrated the fundamentals and then gave us some simulation assignments on computer to carry out in the lab duration itself. Signals and Systems was considered to be the most difficult one. I was busy doing my the computer simulation. After half an hour, surprisingly, Aditi came to me and requested, "Can you please explain the logic behind this MATLAB program? Actually, I am unable to simulate it."

"Yes, of course," I said.

I started to explain the program with my eyes fixed on her face while she was looking at the program on my computer screen. I could feel her fragrance as I explained to her the complete program. After her doubts had been cleared, she complimented me. Meanwhile, lab period was over and it was lunch time.

So, after the lab period, I realized Aditi was looking tired.

"I'm hopeless in Signals and Systems lab," she said taking a sip from her water bottle.

"No, it's okay. It happens initially, otherwise it's quite an interesting subject, and scoring too," I said.

She finished the water and shook her empty water bottle. "I'm still thirsty," she said.

"Let's go to the college cafeteria," I suggested.

She looked at me, somewhat surprised. I kept a straight face.

"Probably, you will get some water and also some juice there," I said in an innocent tone.

She agreed and we both moved towards the cafeteria.

The cafeteria was packed with students. It took us almost five minutes to get a table. Aditi asked for a juice and I ordered a burger and a cold coffee. I realized both of us hesitated to initiate any conversation. I couldn't talk because I didn't have the confidence. She, being tired, preferred to be quiet.

Meanwhile, the waiter brought us our food. "In Gorakhpur, we used to eat these kinds of burgers in our school's canteen in lunch periods," I tried to initiate the conversation.

"What's Gorakhpur like? I've never been there," she said sipping her juice.

"Not crowded like Delhi, quite simple and peaceful, apart from main markets like Golghar and Cinema Road," I told her.

"I like those simple and peaceful places," she said.

"But, there are some problems, too. Most of the people are not properly educated. Sometimes, there's violence on petty issues. Some people are rich there, but still, most people lead an average life," I said.

Again, there was an awkward silence between us for two minutes. Aditi was silent, I was scared though.

"So you live with your family in Delhi?" I again started to talk.

"Yes, a big family. Parents, uncles, cousins and a brother," she said.

"What do your parents do?" I said.

Usually, an engineering guy should make some fascinating and touching conversation with a girl. But, a shy, introvert and conservative boy like me had little experience to do all that.

"My family is in the diamond business. Earlier, my grandfather used to live in Surat, Gujarat. He started this business there. Later on, we shifted to Delhi with the same business. Now our business is widespread in India as well as abroad," she said.

"You are quite rich, right?" I said with hesitation.

She laughed at my direct conclusion.

"Can I take a bite from your burger?" she asked. "I'm hungry."

I nodded in agreement. I asked the waiter to get another fork for us. But, before he could get one, she picked up my fork and took a bite.

"Where do you live in Gorakhpur?" she asked.

"University Road," I said.

"Nice, tell me more about you and your family," she said.

"You will probably find it boring," I said.

"No, it's not like that. I always prefer to listen," she said.

I looked at her face. She seemed genuinely interested. I told her about my life back home, revolving around my mother, father, friends, and school. I also told her about my passion for writing. Meanwhile, Aditi finished her juice and I realized that I had been talking for the past five minutes.

"Oh, you are getting bored," I said. *Control yourself, Keshav and keep quiet for a few minutes*, I said to myself.

Aditi smiled.

We walked out of the cafeteria to the main gate. She stepped inside the car and sat down. She rolled down the window to say goodbye.

"Okay Keshav! Bye, see you later," she said.

"Okay, bye," I replied.

The car drove off and I moved towards my hostel with a broad smile on my face.

7

Words are the route to your heart

Gradually, my bond with Aditi grew stronger. Aditi was now more comfortable talking to me. She was impressed with my academic brilliance. I was happier, more cheerful and smiled a lot more than before.

Girls are always interested in friendship, but boys use their friendship to climb the ladder of love.

When a girl takes care of a boy, he thinks it's love. When a boy takes care of a girl, she thinks it's friendship.

We started having more conversations, either through messages or over phone calls.

I always wished that our conversation would continue for longer – maybe forever.

As days passed, I became fonder of her. I did not know whether it was just infatuation or love, but I liked her for sure.

We used to hang out a lot in the college cafeteria. It was a new world altogether. And I loved each moment of it. We bonded with each other quickly.

The fact that engineering was not her first choice like me brought us even closer.

She had become a part of my daily routine now. Aditi's smiling face was always in my mind.

After a few weeks, I realized that Aditi wasn't just a crush. I was in love with her. But I was not sure about her feelings.

She used to sing a lot while we were together. I always asked her to sing '*Zindagi kaisi hai paheli haye, kabhi to hansaye, kabhi to rulaye…*' for me. This was my favourite song.

I was overwhelmed to know that Aditi too was a devotee of Lord Narayana.

I used to make notes for her and would help her in studies.

Aditi was really special in every respect. Her smile was so pure, so auspicious and when she smiled, she made me forget everything else. I used to lose myself in that beautiful smile.

I tried to convince my heart that she was just a friend. But, it was a lie. Deep inside, I was falling in love. She was perfect; perfect for me. One of the best parts in a boy's life: getting a girl as a best friend.

Further, the stupidest thing in the world: Acting like a friend with the person you love!!

8

Why was everything so complicated?

20 October 2012

After our third semester sessionals ended, I decided to go out somewhere with Aditi. For this, I had to convince her a lot and she finally agreed to watch a movie with me. During the movie, I wondered what Aditi thought of me. We spent so much time together, in college and outside too. We shared almost everything with each other. She listened to me patiently, even smiled sometimes. When I asked her about her personal life, she didn't say much. Am I someone special to her or just a friend? I did not understand our relationship. I kept pondering over the fact when Aditi interrupted my thoughts.

"Did you just put your hand on mine?" She was furious.

"Oh, sorry. I put it accidentally," I said earnestly.

"Keshav, you have come here to watch the movie. So, focus on that!" she said, almost yelling at me.

"Okay," I said again. I turned my attention back to the movie.

Meanwhile, she removed her arm from the armrest. She seemed upset, even though she never said a word. She kept watching the film with great interest.

"Is everything okay?" I asked her.

She sipped her drink in silence. We had walked to the food court after the movie.

"Yes, I am fine," she said.

"See, I'm sorry," I said in a soft voice.

"For what?" she said, in a rather surprised tone.

"About placing my hand on yours during the movie," I said.

"No issue, I didn't even remember that," she said.

"Oh," I said, and felt relaxed.

"Let's go to home now, otherwise I'll be too late?" she said.

"Aditi, you never talk about your personal life. Am I only good enough for you to discuss study stuff in college?"

"What do you mean?"

"See, we meet every day in college, study together and spend so much time with each other. But you never share anything important about your personal life," I said.

"I usually don't share much about my life with anyone, Keshav," she said.

"Am I just anyone for you?" I said.

"You are a friend." She smiled and continued, "Well, you are a topper, brilliant student and make excellent notes, better than anyone else. You help me so much in my studies. I have realized that you are very soft spoken and have respect for girls; girls can share their issues with you comfortably. That's why I like you the most and you are my friend."

Friendship is a lovely track, travelled by two, hand in hand, to care, to share, and to forgive.

I remained silent with a straight face.

"Why do you want to know about my personal life?" she asked looking at me.

"I want to know things about you, your family, your ambitions, your future plans and many such things, and it's quite common for friends to know about each other," I said

She laughed, her eyes met mine, "Okay, I will tell you everything about me. Let's go for a walk," she said.

We walked together towards Connaught Place. It was a pleasant evening. I was happy to be in her company.

"Keshav, you know I'm a quiet person, but I want to help others in whatever ways I can. It's my nature. I don't keep bad feelings in my heart for anyone. I always try to be positive in life. So, I have two sides. One is, egoistic, full of attitude. And the other one is, innocent, childish and stupid. So, don't be too quick to judge," Aditi said.

"I understand and appreciate your way of thinking," I praised her.

"Thanks, the actual problem for me is my family, especially my parents. Although my parents love me immensely, they're obsessed with business. They don't care for my dreams and my passion. So, there is an ideology clash between me and my parents," she said.

"That's how most of the parents in India are?" I said.

"You are right, but according to them, I'm supposed to complete engineering and look after my family business along with my brother, get married and leave. The prime aim of my life should be to have kids and shop."

"And that's not what you want to do?" I interfered.

"Yes, by now, it seems you have understood me better than my family. I don't need everybody in my life. I just need a few people like you who truly understand me," she said.

"Sorry, you seem upset. Did something happen recently in your family?" I asked.

"I always try to tell and convince my parents that I am not like other girls. I do not want to live an ordinary life without any passion. Engineering is not my passion. I am doing it because of them. Engineering has been forced upon me. They want me to marry into some rich family as early as possible and live a luxurious life. That is not what I dream of; I want to achieve something on my own. I want to be a singing star, like you want to become an author of repute. This is my dream, my purpose of life," she said in one breath with excitement on her face.

"Wow, great! I understand," I said.

"Yes. That's it. I want to give a meaning to my life. I want to be a famous singer or a rock star. I don't want to marry a billionaire or run a business. I just want to sing in peace, surrounded by passionate people and become a famous singer first in India and then worldwide," she said.

She continued, "You know Keshav, at home, someone once asked me *why you love music so much*? I replied, because it's the only thing that stays when everything and everyone is gone."

"Sounds like you have it all figured out," I said. However, I said to myself *your voice is music to my ears, your smile is beauty to my eyes.*

"Not really. Maybe it's just an escapist fantasy. But I have been singing since my childhood. I also play guitar proficiently. I won so many awards in singing during my school days. Both of us have similar kind of dreams and ambitions in life other than engineering. A life without a goal is such a meaningless life," she said.

"Yes, there is no reason to look back when you have so much to look forward to with your ambitions and dreams," I said.

"I'm learning to love myself and it's the hardest thing I've ever done."

The sun was setting, and the sky turned from orange to dark grey. She continued to tell me about her dreams, her calling, her passion of life i.e. singing and guitar.

"Anyway, I like and respect your dreams, Aditi. You are not an ordinary girl. You want to live the life of your dreams. I also want to do the same. It's not unreal, we can achieve our ambitions in life with extraordinary hard work," I said.

She smiled. "Nothing is simple for a girl in a family like mine," she said.

"Aditi, when you follow or choose any good path, you always get obstacles in the beginning. It's not easy to bring good changes. It takes time and efforts, but everyone will remember you for being unique," I said.

"Yes, exactly, I also believe in the same philosophy."

"Aditi, you are smart, hard-working, and ambitious. You have a great future ahead," I motivated her.

"Yes, a dream doesn't come true automatically. It demands firm determination, hard work and commitment. Anyway, thanks for the compliments!"

We walked in silence for a few minutes.

"I am feeling better now," she said after a while.

"What…?"

She looked at me. The last rays of the daylight tinted her face orange, making her look even more beautiful. I wanted to hug her.

Some girls don't need makeup to look beautiful, they just need to smile. Aditi was one of them.

"I feel better after talking to you. Deep conversations with someone who understands you are everything. Thanks, Keshav." She smiled.

Aditi was right. A ten-minute conversation with the person you like or love is enough to keep you happy the entire day.

She said further, "Keshav, you know, sometimes in life, you find a special friend; someone who changes your life just by being a part of it. Someone who makes you laugh until you can't stop; someone who makes you believe that there is really something good in the world. I see exactly that kind of best friend in you."

I felt elated instantly.

Meanwhile, the sun vanished and the road became dark. There was definitely something special for me in that evening. Her skin glowed in the amber lights of Connaught Place. I took a chance and held her hand.

"Another accident?" she said, but did not pull her hand away. We laughed together.

She spoke again, "Even my brother is the same. Everyone sides with my parents."

She continued to talk and I continued to listen, even though my entire attention was on how lovely her hand felt in mine.

Though she didn't know about my feelings for her, yet I experienced the feeling of true love for the first time in my life. It seemed both of us were soul-mates with the same kind of feelings, thought process and dreams in life. Whatever our souls were made of, her and mine were the same.

Love is a very unique feeling, and if it is from both sides, then nothing is sweeter than that. It is said that the spaces between our fingers were created so that another's can fill them in.

While leaving, she hugged me for the first time. It was something special for me.

Little hugs can dry big tears.

After our first date; we started to spend even more time together.

"How's the food in the hostel?" she said taking a bite from her lunch box.

We were sitting in the college lawn during our lunch break.

"Not as good as we have at home," I said.

"Keshav, you know, I bought a new guitar," she said in excitement.

"Oh, very nice, but you already have many as far as I know," I said.

"Yeah, but it's new and the best one in my stock." She smiled.

"Aditi, you know students around here talk about us," I said.

"So? Let them. As long as we know there is nothing between us," she said carelessly.

"What do you mean by nothing?" I asked.

She remained silent.

"I really like you, Aditi. You mean so much to me. You are the reason I've survived in this place," I said with slight nervousness on my face.

"Keshav, you are my best friend and I don't care what people talk about us. Please appreciate our friendship. We are true friends without any physical interaction. You please don't do anything that spoils it. Although I live in Delhi, I'm very traditional as well as modern in my beliefs."

I kept my face straight.

She further tried to convince me, "Life can give us a number of friends! But, only a true friend like you can give me a beautiful life! I can talk to you about any damn time and burst into laughter or tears. I know that I won't be judged. I think every girl in the world wants a guy with whom she can really be herself."

"Yes, I agree." I said to her, but in my mind, "But, a life without you is not a life for me."

"Okay, love is beautiful because it is controlled by the hearts. But, friendship is even more beautiful because it is a feeling that takes care of another heart," she again said.

I was quiet.

She looked at me for a few seconds, smiled, shook her head and hugged me.

While returning to hostel, I vowed to create a balance between my friendship with Aditi and my career, my ambitions, so as to enjoy both the aspects of life.

9

One step closer

It was 6 November – her birthday. I wanted to make our friendship stronger. I wanted to make her realize what she meant to me. My classmates arranged a small birthday party for Aditi in class during the lunch period.

I also wished her in the morning itself.

After attending the classes, Aditi and I went to the college lawn in the evening. It was a stunning evening. The birds were going home and they filled the air with a happy tune.

As soon as we reached the lawn, she asked me, "Where is my birthday gift?"

"How are you so sure that I bought a gift for you?" I said, surprised.

"How can my best friend not give me a gift today?" she said softly.

I was mesmerized with these amiable words and felt like kissing her, but I controlled my emotions.

"Aditi, I didn't expect that I would be able to meet you today."

"Why?"

"You know, many of our classmates, students from other classes and so many seniors have a massive crush on you. You are more than just a face for them. They kept on rushing to you to extend birthday wishes the entire day."

"Might be. But, you are my true companion. Nobody can take your place."

I couldn't speak.

Aditi felt the silence in the atmosphere. She held my hand and changed the topic, "Give me my birthday gift."

As the fluffy clouds flowed in the light blue sky, the breeze touched both of us. My heart raced a little faster with every touch. Suddenly a light drizzle started.

I opened my bag and gave her a chocolate, along with flowers.

"Oh! Nice chocolate, but I think you have something else, too," she said peeping inside my bag.

She was so curious that she gave the chocolate back to me and flipped the card open.

"Wow! What a nice birthday card," she exclaimed, blissfully.

What's so special about this card? I wondered. My heart began beating uncontrollably.

We shared the chocolate. There was definitely something special about that evening.

"Keshav, I should go now. I've to go for a birthday dinner with my family," she said.

"Okay. Wish you a very happy birthday again!" I said, while shaking hands with her.

She sat in the car and said, "Good night, Keshav."

I said to myself, *you've made this day a special day just by being you. There's no one in the world quite like you, and I like you just the way you are.*

10

A gifted singing star

My friends Vivaan and Reyansh had been very passionate about extracurricular activities since their school days; they emerged as the cultural events coordinator in DTU in a short time. So, they had been exceptionally busy recently. The college fest was round the corner and both of them were the main members of the core organizing committee of the fest.

On the day of the fest, all the students were very excited. Everyone was wearing their best dresses and impressive outfits, including me. I cheered up looking at the joyful canopy at the entrance gate. Soon, the main stage events began and the best of girls in DTU started walking the ramp in shiny clothes. It was a magnificent sight. Guys were hooting for them while the girls smiled and ignored them.

Once all the ramp walks were done, it was time for some performances. First a dance group took the stage. And then came Aditi for her solo singing event.

"Ladies and gentlemen, we have Aditi to play in front of you this evening. She is an upcoming singing talent. I am sure you will love her. So everybody, a big hand for Aditi," Vivaan announced on the stage.

Aditi played the famous song *'Brother Louie' by Modern Talking*. The song seemed to come out perfect on the mike. She was just playing her own guitar with background music. The song ended and the crowd applauded, but the reaction was not as superlative as I had imagined. To me, that was one of the best performances of Aditi. Aditi had fifteen minutes on the stage. So, she geared up to play another song. I was hopping her second song would be better. She tightened her grip on the guitar and plucked the string of her guitar to announce she was starting.

'*Chura liya hai tumne jo dil ko...*' she sang and the crowd erupted.

They all loved it.

Everybody came up on their feet and started swaying with the music. It was more than evident that Aditi was a hit in this audience. The song ended and the ovation went on for a while.

The crowd was shouting, "Once more, once more!" Clearly, Aditi was a hit.

Aditi turned around to check with Vivaan if she could play the song once again. Vivaan nodded in agreement. Aditi picked her guitar again and went for another one.

At the end of the performance, Aditi stepped down the stage and came towards me. I congratulated her. She hugged me.

Aditi was the singing star of that evening.

11

Special moments

It was a beautiful Wednesday evening. As the big popcorn clouds seemed to be dancing in the sky, with a tinge of pink somewhere in between, they looked like a dream. I felt that these were the most perplexing clouds I had ever seen.

"Hey, I reached fifteen minutes ago. Where are you?" It was Aditi.

"I am just reaching in five minutes, in an auto right now," I said. As I reached Vasant Kunj, I found Aditi waiting for me.

"Does this always happen or are you intentionally late today?" Aditi sneered at me.

"No, I got late due to a traffic jam," I said.

We walked together a few hundred metres down the road before settling in a cafeteria.

We looked a perfect pair from every aspect; be it physique, complexion or height.

Weather was a bit cold that day. The cafeteria was moderately occupied for a Wednesday evening. The instrumental music in the background set the mood and atmosphere.

I couldn't take my eyes off Aditi. Overall, the cafeteria was a bright happy place and high on love.

We started talking about various things.

I also told her about the fiction book I was working on and she was fascinated by it.

"Wow!" she leaned forward. "You're writing a book. That is so cool! What inspired you to write one?"

"I was inspired by you and your passion towards the guitar and singing," I said.

She gazed at me for some time, slowly sipping her coffee.

"If I had to live the life of my dreams, I would have to find time for my passion against all odds in life, as you are doing," I said.

She looked at me proudly, and smiled.

Problem with Boys: They can make you believe that they love you, even when they don't...

Problems with girls: They can make you believe that they don't love you, even when they really do.

After spending some more time, we came out. As soon as we came out, it started raining. The sky was cloudy and dark. We waited there; however, Aditi was enjoying the rain. Her hair was soaked. I passed my handkerchief to her to dry her hair.

She replied, "No, I'm fine, I forgot mine today."

"Aditi take it, your face is too wet," I emphasized.

She took it, dried her hair and wiped her face gently with the handkerchief.

"Thank you!! I'll return it tomorrow, after washing."

"No, it's alright." I said with a smile on my face and took the handkerchief from her.

Aditi shared a special bond with nature and felt elated. She loved getting wet in the rain, the simple joys of life. She always found rain so enchanting. According to her, during rains, everything looked more alive, fresh green, beautiful, like someone has sprinkled water on all the impurities around, making everything vibrant, colourful, a bliss for the eyes.

"It's so amazing to walk in the rain, isn't it?" Aditi asked, watching the people who were walking by.

"I have not experienced it yet," I said gently and followed her eyes to look at the same people.

"Seriously?"

"Yes, I have never walked in the rain," I took the last bite of popcorn.

My words brought a pleasant smile on her calm face. Walking on the road, Aditi was sharing moments from her school days. Her eyes were sparkling with joy at that time. At one point, due to water logged on the road, she held my hand. At that moment, I felt even more connected with Aditi, not just by a tender touch, but by an invisible bond of affection. I felt like I was flying.

I said to myself, *you may hold my hand for a while. But you hold my heart forever. I want to hold your hand, laugh at your jokes, walk by your side, snuggle on the couch, look into your eyes, talk about whatever and kiss your lips every single day.*

She had become my inspiration

I was overwhelmed by my feelings for her. I wanted to tell her that she was everything to me; my world, my inspiration, my motivation and many things which are even indescribable.

I couldn't imagine my life without her. In every part of my life, I wanted her beside me. Though it was a dream that may or may not be successful, but it did not matter.

Aditi was, in fact, a super optimist. She always used to inspire me to achieve my goals. Whenever she realized that I was going out of track from my passion, from my studies, she would instill confidence in me saying, "If you have thought about something, then Lord Narayana has already planned the same for you. Just work towards achieving it."

She herself used to follow the same principle towards her dreams.

12

Can't live without you

My feelings for Aditi were increasing day by day. I was becoming more passionate about her. I thought I should propose to her, which I should have said much earlier.

But how would I initiate? It had been a long time. I was brooding over it. Then I decided to write my feelings on a paper, but did not intend to give the same to her.

I wrote many pages, and soon I had a thick bundle. I read it many times. I didn't even know how many times I edited and rewrote it to make it more impressive and meaningful.

I also thought of expressing myself through messages, but couldn't gather the courage to do it.

After our third semester was over, I decided to convey my feelings to her.

It was the last day of the third semester exams. I wanted to meet Aditi. Meanwhile, Vivaan and Reyansh came towards me.

"What's up bro? How was the paper?" Vivaan enquired.

"Good," I replied.

"Let's go out for lunch. After all, the exams finally got over," Reyansh always had some plan in mind.

"I am heading to Lucknow tomorrow. So, let's go for dinner tonight," Vivaan agreed.

"I will let you know," I was not sure.

"Do you have any other plan with Aditi?" Reyansh had an impish smile on his face.

"No plan as of now," I responded.

I saw her leaving.

"Guys, I will catch you later. I need to speak to her, now."

I ran towards her. She was not very far away from me. I followed her quickly.

By the time I approached her, she was near the car. She looked back.

"Hey Aditi!" I greeted.

"Hello Keshav! How was your paper?" she asked.

"It was good. What about yours?"

"Excellent."

"Are you going home?" I asked.

"Yes, tell me, what's the matter?" she asked, curiously.

"Nothing much. So, what's your plan for the holidays? Are you going somewhere?" I asked her, hesitatingly.

"No, I don't have any plans. But, let's see. How about you?"

"Oh, okay. If you are free, can we meet for dinner tonight?"

"Dinner? No, it's not possible. Some guests are coming at home and it is not possible to go out at night," she said, softly.

"Okay, no problem. Lunch tomorrow?" I kept trying.

"Lunch? Okay. Would tomorrow noon work?" she asked.

"Yes, it's okay," I said.

"So, let's meet for lunch."

I reached the restaurant thirty minutes before time. She entered the restaurant fifteen minutes late, wearing her most favourite white top and blue jeans.

"Hey, how are you?" She smiled.

"Hello! I am good. You are late." I started the conversation with a complaint.

"Yeah, I was busy with some guests at home as I told you yesterday."

"Okay, let's order something." I didn't know if I was in a rush or nervous.

"Yes, sure."

We ordered food and then continued the conversation.

"I wanted to talk to you for a long time, but unfortunately, couldn't get the chance," I regretted.

"Yes, we were busy with the exam preparation. How did it go for you?"

"Good. I will get excellent marks yet again," I replied.

She was quite impressed with my confidence.

"How about you?" I asked.

"Let's see. It was not bad. I am more concerned about my singing practice which I couldn't do for the last one month."

"You may practice now, in the semester break."

"Yeah, I'll utilize this time sincerely," she said. "But, what about your book? Have you written some more chapters?" she asked.

"Yeah, I'm trying to write," I tried to look away.

"Keshav, it's bad! You are out of your track, you should not give a back seat to your passion. Please make a balance between your writing and engineering, like me," she scolded me.

"Okay, I'll write some more during the semester break," I said.

"That's a good guy," she said with smile on her face.

I kept quiet. I said to myself, *it's because of you Aditi, I get out of track because I cannot forget you even for a minute.*

I was a little anxious. I was in a fix, whether I should express my feelings to her or not. What if she felt upset? I wanted to confess my feelings to her. But was it too early? Was I rushing? I brooded a lot on this, but finally decided to give this a go.

Meanwhile, the waiter brought the lunch. He served us and walked away.

Aditi continued, "Let's eat!"

"Aditi, I want to say something," I said.

"Tell me Keshav. What is it?" she asked.

"Actually…" I stammered.

"What?" she asked again.

She realized that I was nervous.

I mustered some courage to speak further.

"Hey, I know it could feel a bit awkward, but I had to say this. Don't take it in the wrong way. I am sorry, if you find it weird," I continued the conversation.

"No problem, tell me," she interrupted me with her evergreen smile.

"Please don't interrupt me. It would wipe off the courage that I have gathered," I said.

She looked deep into my eyes. This time, she became serious.

I started, "Aditi, I am an emotional person. I love to speak my heart out. You are someone with whom I want to spend more time… I guess my entire life. I want to be with you till my last breath. I often smile for no reason and it's because of you. I would like to confess that whenever I am with you, I feel complete. I am sure I am in love with you. I strongly feel that you are my soul-mate. My love for you is timeless and endless. I cannot imagine my life in your absence. You are like the breath of air that I need to live, the drop of water in a thirsty desert.

"To meet you was my destiny, to befriend you was my free will. But to fall in love with you…. It was not in my control. Will you be my life companion?" I further said.

First, she remained silent with disbelief. She was dazed.

She took a deep breath and looked at me. I was dying to hear her answer. My gaze was fixed on her, feeling crushed.

Did I ruin everything in haste? Should I have taken more time? It wasn't that I didn't believe in myself.

She replied, "Keshav, listen carefully. It may sound a little weird but the fact is that I don't believe in love before marriage. You are a really good friend of mine and I am happy to be your friend, but I don't love you. In fact, I don't love anyone in that way. I don't believe in it. So, sorry to hurt you, but we can just be good friends, nothing else. I earlier told you that we will remain best friends without any physical aspect between us.

"I don't believe in these love stories. Don't spoil our true friendship. I have already told you about my ambition in life. Both of us have to move forward in our respective lives and achieve our dreams. I'll again advise you to focus on your studies and your dream in life. I am saying this from the core of my heart. I will be the first person to congratulate you on, achieving your dreams in life," she said, choking.

She continued, "I don't want a relationship; it holds you back. I want a best friend. Somebody who I can trust completely. Relationships just aren't for me, but a friendship, I'll take that."

I kept quiet and tried to look away. I was shattered. I didn't expect this from her. This was not easy to bear. It was painful, but I didn't say anything to her.

We finished our lunch. Even the delicious food left a sour taste in my mouth after this conversation.

"Let's move! I am getting late," she said, sternly.

"Yes, sure," I said.

"So, what else?" I asked.

"Nothing. I will go home. Mom must be waiting for me," she seemed a little upset.

"Okay," I said.

She sat inside her car and was gone.

I stood there looking at the departing car until it disappeared.

I was amused with her simplicity, her politeness, and her emotional words. It showed how much she cared for me. I also came to know how much she was concerned about my career here in DTU and my dreams of becoming an author. She was also very firm about her ambitions and did not want to waste time. She wanted to see both of us reaching heights in life. That's why she became so upset on my proposal. Definitely, she was a different kind of girl.

I started to walk toward my hostel. I was feeling desolate and needed to talk to someone. I felt like crying, yelling and shouting, but controlled myself, somehow.

After what seemed like a long time, there was a beep on my cell phone.

She had texted. *"Hope, you reached your hostel safely. Take care of yourself in the long journey to Gorakhpur. Good night."*

It gave me immense pleasure and satisfaction. At least she still cared for me. Somewhere in my heart, I knew that she too liked me, but there was something which she was hiding. *I would surely convince her one day*, I said to myself

When I was leaving for Gorakhpur for my semester holidays, I had decided not to think about her anymore.

13

A memorable day

Our fourth semester had already started when I returned to DTU.

I hadn't talked to Aditi after the proposal episode as I was afraid of annoying her again.

I was not sure if she would want to study with me anymore. However, to my surprise, she did. She came and sat beside me as usual in the lawn.

We studied without much conversation.

Today, she focused on studies like a soldier does in combat with an enemy. I had decided to be her best friend as per her advice, didn't want to cross any line, now.

She was lost in her thoughts. Noticing the sullen look on her face, I asked, "What brings the frown on your face?"

"Nothing."

"Come on, I know something is going on in your superlative brain. Speak up," I said trying to read her mind.

"I was just thinking about something.," she said turning her face in another direction.

"I am sorry for hurting you so much that day, okay?" I said.

"It's fine," she said, "Let's not talk about it again."

"I should not have proposed like that. Now, I have clearly understood your philosophy in life. I'll also strive hard to achieve heights in life and fulfil my dreams, like you," I said.

"Friendship is all about understanding and being understood. Sorry, I also overreacted, we are still best friends," she said.

"Really? It's okay now?" I said.

"It's okay, no issue. Keshav, I repeatedly ask you to concentrate on your goals. I will be sad if you don't achieve any one of them. This is a the precious time, both of us can craft our careers," she said.

"Thanks, I will do my best."

"Listen, before I forget, I have to invite you to a party," she said.

"Party?"

"Yes," she said.

"Where is it?" I asked.

"Next Saturday, my house," she said.

"Your house?" I asked.

"Yes, the party is at my place," she said.

"That means you're making me meet your parents?" I asked, surprised.

"Yeah, why? There are going to be lots of people there. It's a party," she said.

"Oh, but what is the occasion?" I said.

"My parents' silver jubilee," she said.

"Wow, that's great!"

"Actually, my brother and I made this plan. Both of us want to celebrate it with full enthusiasm. Luckily, we have family friends and relatives available in town," she said.

I nodded in agreement.

"Okay! I will come," I said.

"Bye." She stood up, hugged me and walked off.

I looked into the mirror to see my reflection and discover the changes I had gone through in the past one-and-a-half years of my college time had flown so fast and brought so many changes.

I dressed up well. It was a special day after all.

Evenings in February are quite chilly in Delhi. It took me a cab ride and some walking to get to New Friends Colony in South Delhi.

"108, New Friends Colony." I saw the sign which merely stated 'Kohli'. I approached the guards.

Guards asked a few things. Once convinced, they let me go inside. A maid gestured for me to a garden where loud music and a waft of cool breeze greeted me. The garden was lit up with small fairy lights. White-gloved servers manned a buffet and a bar counter.

I looked around for Aditi.

"Hey, Keshav!" I heard her perky voice.

I saw Aditi waving at me from a distance. She walked towards me. Her face looked even prettier than it did every day.

She hugged me like she always did. I felt elated.

"Why are you so late, Keshav?" she asked, holding my hand.

"Took a while to figure out your house," I replied.

"I told you I would send a car," she said. "Anyway, come!"

We walked towards the pool where she introduced me to her friends. She was still holding my hand.

After formal introduction, Aditi asked me, "Come, Keshav, meet my parents."

Aditi's parents wore well-ironed clothes with immaculate accessories. The couple was in their early fifties.

"Aditi, where were you beta?" Mr Kohli said. He put his arm around his daughter. "Everyone has been asking for you."

"Dad, I want you to meet Keshav, my best friend from DTU. I told you about him," Aditi said.

Mr Kohli looked at me and smiled.

"Hello, Keshav," Mr Kohli said. He shook my hand, vigorously.

"Good to meet you, sir," I said.

"Where do you belong to, beta?" Mr Kohli asked me.

"Sir, I belong to Gorakhpur," I replied.

"I am happy to meet you; Aditi has told us about you several times. You are a hard working guy and a topper of DTU. She is very proud of you. She always says that Keshav and I are on the same frequency and both of us are equally ambitious to get something special in life. She is sure that one day you will become a renowned author," he continued.

I felt proud. Aditi was also looking at me, with a smile on her face.

"And that's my Mom," Aditi said turning towards her mom.

Aditi's mother smiled and folded her hands. I wished her with a namaste too. A waiter arrived with a tray of drinks. He served cold drinks to all of us.

I extended my warm wishes to her parents and later she introduced me to her brother Gaurav. He was polite and soft spoken.

I was highly impressed by the etiquette of every member of the family.

Meanwhile all the guests had arrived and Aditi and her parents were busy welcoming them. Gradually, the place was teeming with family and friends.

Everybody greeted Aditi's parents. After dinner, guests assembled in the garden and requested Mr Kohli to give a small speech on the occasion.

"I am quite happy and content to welcome you all here. Never expected this. It's indeed a big day in my life when we are celebrating twenty-five years of our married life. Thanks to my wife Sarika for supporting me in all these years. It would never have been possible to achieve all these without her love and support. I think you can achieve everything in life if you have an understanding partner. Spouse is the most important building pillar of anyone's life. I am glad that I have one. I am happy to see my children Gaurav and Aditi organizing a party for all of us. Love you both. Thank you all for your presence," he finished his speech with folded hands and wet eyes.

It was an emotional moment for Aditi and Gaurav. Mrs and Mr Kohl hugged Gaurav and Aditi and I was touched to see such a loving family.

14

The world seemed so beautiful

As time passed, Aditi and I became closer than before. I would often go to Aditi's house and became familiar with her parents and brother. They knew I was exceptionally well in studies and I was the one whom their daughter could easily trust.

One Saturday evening, Aditi called me to her house to spend some time together and then hang out in the evening. I was elated and full of joy. I was happy to spend time with her.

I reached her house. I met her parents. After formal exchange of wishes, I went to Aditi's room and knocked on the door, "Aditi."

"Come inside, Keshav, the door is open."

I pushed the door open and realized that she was in the bath.

"Make yourself comfortable, Keshav. I will be ready in ten minutes," she screamed from the glass cubicle covered with white curtains.

My brain started to erupt with some naughty thoughts and to divert my mind, I switched on the TV.

"Keshav …." she called again. "I forgot my towel outside, could you please pass that to me?" she sounded very seductive.

I thought that she too would have felt quite embarrassed asking like this. While passing the towel, I tried my best not to look at her, but I got a glimpse of her through the mirror on the opposite wall; it was purely unintentional.

She came out shortly afterwards.

Active, charged, excited, nervous, whatever adjectives you can imagine, were not enough to count my emotion at that moment. Her beauty had made me speechless again and I actually gulped before I could say anything.

She was looking stunning. Her body was covered with water droplets and her long and dense hair were enough to make me get lost in them. "Are you okay?" she asked adjusting her dress with her hand.

I smiled back. I was feeling shy.

"Yes, shall we move now?" I said, pointing my hand towards the door.

"First, I will show you my new guitar, after that we'll go outside," she said.

"Okay," I said.

"So, you have bought another guitar?" I asked her.

"Yes, I can't live without music and my singing practice. I play guitar and sing a song whenever I get time at home," she said.

"How did you learn guitar and singing initially?" I asked.

"Initially, I learnt it from the internet! Where else, and then in singing classes…" she answered.

Aditi started playing guitar. She touched the first string and there was no looking back. She forgot that I was sitting there and she played a tune which I had never heard before. It had to be her composition. For the first time, I realized, Aditi was a phenomenal talent. I felt she would be a rage; whichever stage she would step on. She was a genius. Her fingers moved faster than I had ever imagined.

Just then, her phone rang and broke the flow.

"Was that okay, Keshav?" she asked me.

"It was fantastic. I am glad and proud of you. I can predict today; you are going to be a singing star in future," I said excitedly.

"Thanks for the complement. But, I am still learning. Anyway, let's move," she said.

We drove to the Laxmi Narayan Temple, also known as the Birla Mandir. It's one of the cleanest and most beautiful temples in Delhi – an absolutely beautiful temple with stunning architecture and amazing statues.

"Are you coming here for the first time?" Aditi asked me.

"Yes, and you?"

"Actually, I have come here a number of times. I have seen this temple since my childhood. It is a good picnic spot, too," Aditi said.

The atmosphere inside the temple was peaceful, and the design ensured the climate inside was nice and cool – a massive contrast to outside. We spent almost an hour there. Prayer is the best wireless connection to god.

I talked to the Lord, "Dear god, from the bottom of my heart, I want to thank you for being with me all the way, for loving me, for forgiving me, for healing me and never leaving me alone."

After the prayer, we went to have food.

"Tell me something more about you, Keshav," Aditi said to me, as we were waiting for food.

"You already know everything. There is nothing more to know about me," I said.

"No, I mean, I know everything about you after I met you. Tell me something from the time before I met you," she clarified.

"What more do you want to know? My father is a government teacher, who has worked for several colleges in Gorakhpur. He has always loved his work and he wants to be good at whatever he does. And he has done pretty well too," I explained.

"And your mom?"

"My mom is the most adjusting and loving person in the world. Whatever my dad says is acceptable to her. She is the sweetest lady ever," I said.

"This looks awesome," she said, while capturing a picture of the food that was served.

"So, can we eat now, if your photo sessions are over?" I said and took her phone.

My life seemed to flow smoothly since the time she had come in my life. She had made it so beautiful that I myself was amazed. She would hug me so tightly that nobody else could ever do. Her emotional feelings would fill me with elation, taking me to a state of levitation.

"Keshav, let's go now." Her perky voice disturbed my thoughts.

"Okay," I said.

"How'll you go back to the hostel? It's already 9 p.m.," Aditi asked me, looking concerned.

"I'll go by an auto or a cab."

"Let me drop you at your hostel first, and then I'll go home."

"It's okay, Aditi. I'll go, no problem at all."

"See, if my parents come to know that I left you on the road at this time, they'll kill me. They are too concerned for you."

"Oh, is it? What did they say?"

"They always ask me to check about you, whether you have reached hostel safely or not?"

"Okay," I was amused to know this.

So, Aditi dropped me at my hostel that night. She didn't leave until I safely entered the hostel.

15

Would walk a million miles for you

Our third year also went very well. I topped yet again. Aditi was the first one to congratulate me; she would be so happy, as if she had topped herself. I had earned high regards from Aditi and her parents. I used to assume her as my soul-mate because both of us had several things in common. Our thought process would also match and we would read each other's minds and understand each other. However, she still used to consider me as her best friend only, with no other relations. Whenever she felt that I was going out of track, she used to advise me to not think of love and such kind of stuff before you achieve your dreams. She herself always followed her philosophy of life and practiced hard in singing.

During the third year, she became popular among students as a singer and went to perform in cultural functions of some nearby schools and engineering colleges. She also took part in various inter-state singing competitions and bagged various awards. Whenever she would go in other schools and colleges to perform, her parents were worried for her. They used to advise her not to go alone to perform in the shows.

"Either go with your brother or Keshav, don't go alone," said her father.

However, she used to take me with her in all her shows. She used to feel comfortable and safe in my company and her parents were also assured that their daughter was in the company of a gentleman. Sometimes, we had to stay in school, colleges' guest houses. I would enjoy all such events as we would spend more quality time together.

The bond between me and Aditi grew even stronger with time. Everything was going smoothly. We were enjoying the quality time we spent together in college and while accompanying her during her performances.

We were in the final year now. By now, Aditi had become a popular singer in North India. She was often invited for various shows in several states; Rajasthan and Himachal in particular, where she performed exceptionally well. This became possible because of her dedication and determination, endless nights of hard work and erratic schedule.

One day we were sitting in the college lawn, discussing about future prospects.

"So, what have you decided about your future after completing final year?" I asked her.

"Nothing special, I would go along with my passion and become a national level singer first," she replied.

"That means you would not do jobs after B. Tech?"

She laughed.

"No, not at all... My parents want that I should extend my family business with my brother. So, either I will take over business or choose to go along with my dreams."

"What about you?" she asked me.

"Although I also want to pursue my dream of becoming an author, but, first I will have to look for a job after B. Tech because I want to see my parents happy at home," I replied.

"Okay, but after settling down in a job, within a year, you can realize your passion, simultaneously," she said.

"Yes, I can. Aditi, you are very firm about your career, your dreams, but what about your personal life?" I asked.

"I have not decided yet," she said.

"But, we have been spending good times with each other for the last two years. What will you say about that?" I asked her.

"We are just best friends, nothing else. I have told you several times," she said.

She continued, "Friendship between a boy and a girl is a lot stronger than love."

I kept quiet for a few moments.

"Aditi, don't you think, those common things make us soul-mates; such soul-mates that like and support each other and so can spend a life together? I have always accompanied you in each event, just like your shadow, without desiring anything in return. Everyone presumes us as partners in life. Even your parents and brother see us like that. I have observed such feelings for us in your parents' eyes," I tried to make her realize about our relationship.

"Keshav, I am grateful to you for the efforts you have put in for me. I can't forget your true care and affection for me. Indeed, you have been my shadow in my struggle while performing in schools and colleges. But, I don't understand this love. What I've understood is that you are more than my best buddy. Once we finish our engineering, achieve our dreams altogether and settle into our respective lives, we'll definitely talk to our parents for future prospects. But till then, we'll be best friends, nothing more than that. I'm not the kind of a girl to first fall in love, experience the relationship and then decide whether or not to marry. Love and marriage is the same thing for me, actually," she said in one breath.

"I don't mean that," I said.

"So why can't you just stick to what we discussed earlier? Just best friends."

I remained silent.

"Keshav, according to me, friendship is the sweetest form of love. So when I say I'll be your friend 'till the end', it's as good as saying, I'll keep you in my heart until its very last beat," she tried to explain me.

I felt annoyed and turned away from her.

My eyes welled up. Aditi held my hand and asked me, "Keshav, I want you to look into my eyes and see only me."

I turned my face towards her and could hardly control my tears.

"Look into my eyes and feel a determination to achieve my dreams in life. I want the same firmness in your eyes for your dreams. I don't want you to drift away from your goals for such silly things. All these issues, we'll settle later on. Never let your emotions overpower your intelligence."

I couldn't speak.

"Protect your dreams, Keshav, because it's all you have," she again said. "My dear, friendship is always better than a relationship. A sweet friendship refreshes the soul. Love is not only made for lovers. It is also for friends who love each other better than lovers. A true friend is very hard to find, difficult to leave and impossible to forget."

"My worst fear is losing you," I could hardly say.

She smiled and suddenly put my hand on her heart and said, "Dear best friend, no one will replace you in my life, I promise. Friendship may turn into love, but love will never turn into friendship. Please understand the deep meaning of these words,"

"Are you okay now?" she asked still holding my hand.

"It's okay for me now, no issue," I said.

16

In the blink of an eye

During my final year, I used to go to college just to meet Aditi. She was my first love and it had been my dream to be with her forever. In the final year, students had to prepare for campus placement and other competitive exams like GATE, in addition to college exams.

I used to think of different ways to confess my feelings in front of her, but couldn't have courage to do so, as I was afraid of losing my friendship with her.

However, during the most important phase of my career in the final year, I faced the most difficult time of my life.

My relationship with Aditi underwent a sea change within a few days. Suddenly, my fortune turned upside-down and left me stunned with disbelief, grief and sorrows. Actually, an untoward incident happened in Bhaskaracharya Hostel one night. There was a birthday celebration going on. All my friends were also invited in the celebration. During the party, some guys passed lewd comments about me and Aditi. Vivaan and Reyansh interfered and advised them not to talk loose. However, there was no stopping the disgusting comments from their side; and soon a fight erupted between them. Hostel wardens and some other students tried to stop the fight.

Next day, this was the main news in the entire campus. For me and Aditi, it was hard to believe. Both of us had become infamous for no reason, within a day.

A discipline committee held a meeting and all the culprits were punished. Our Dean also called me and Aditi. He advised both of us to focus on our studies rather than strengthening our friendship as we were in final year now. Further, he called Aditi's parents and advised them to council her daughter to avoid any scuffle among students, due to her. This was so disrespectful for Aditi and her parents. However, Aditi and her parents resisted against all this in front of the Dean and the discipline committee, but, the sad part was that even our faculty also had the same kind of beliefs about us.

For the next few days, Aditi didn't come to college.

She rejoined college after one week and that too in a completely different mood. It seemed as if she was advised hard by her parents to concentrate on her studies, leaving everything else behind and complete her B. Tech degree without any further tussle. Looking at Aditi's face in class, I also felt she was hurt due to that event in the hostel.

Aditi tried to avoid me in class as well as in other parts of college. She was angry to know that I had told everybody that both of us were in a physical relationship and were to marry. She assumed that I had deliberately done that.

However, I knew in my heart that I hadn't done any such thing. How could I stop other students from thinking and spreading rumours? It was a baseless rumour spread by some mischievous students. I was completely numb with shock.

It was a tough situation for me, but it was something that had to happen. It was the regret, which was the worst kind of pain. Yeah, guilt is bad and sadness is bad too, but regret over your mistake is a sick combination of both, especially if that mistake means losing the person you love.

I decided to go to Aditi and apologize for my mistake – the mistake of popularizing our friendship as a love affair among all the students, according to her.

She was looking grave. It was visible from her eyes that she was getting annoyed because of me. But I kept watching her. Her face looked tense, with no smile and then our eyes met. But she looked at me, glazed. There was no hint of a smile on her face. She stood up, and moved to another side.

In the past two years, I was so smitten with Aditi and her attraction that I had ignored many friends in my class. They had moved on, leaving me behind with her.

I stood from my seat and went to her, while she was packing her bag, with an annoyed face.

She did not bother to talk, but I could see how uncomfortable she was. I tried to stop her, but she kept moving. I kept following her; she parted from other girls and began walking alone. I took long steps and reached her. I called her from behind. She turned, looked at me and kept walking. I pulled her right hand, holding her from the elbow and came in front of her. She stopped but avoided eye contact.

"I need to talk to you, Aditi." I came straight to the point.

She kept staring at me in anger and then without speaking a word, tried to leave.

I again tried to obstruct her way and said in a loud voice said, "You need to talk to me, Aditi."

But she did not say a single word and kept walking.

"Aditi," I whispered.

She stopped and looked back at me.

"Two minutes, I beg you," I said.

"I don't want to talk to you, at all," she said.

"I'll keep following you until you talk to me," I said.

She glared at me and stood still, her hands balling into fists.

"Okay, what do you want?" she said.

"Listen, I am really, really sorry, It's not my fault."

She remained silent. It seemed as if she was controlling her tears. She was really sad inside.

"Don't waste your time. Sorry is not going to work," she controlled her anger.

"I didn't have any role in that incident, actually. I can't stop students from spreading rumours about us," I pleaded.

"No, it's only you and your notorious friends who told everyone in all the hostels. You converted our friendship into a love affair. I had always warned you because of this reason. Why did you do it? Do you know how it made me feel? I couldn't sleep well. I have not been able to practice singing for the last few days." She stared into my eyes. I looked away.

"Keshav, I trusted you. I told you every time that we are best friends. But you spread it another way in college and the hostels. Everybody is saying that we are in a relationship and what not! Even our faculty seem to have this impression." She was angry and teary eyed.

"I just…" My heart started to sink as I had never seen Aditi in tears. I had always seen her as firm and determined.

"Just what? I have come to know so many things that students said for me in the hostel that night. Now, I do understand everything," she said and turned her face to hide her tears.

"I just… I just like you, Aditi."

"Yeah, right. Indeed a classy way to show affection. I wonder how you would think of me in your mind."

"I wanted to be close to you. Never let you go. It's my useless friends, they have hyped it," I said.

"That means you discussed everything about us with your friends?" She was furious.

"Not everything but, sometimes ..."

Before I could respond, she said, "I'm going to say something now. Listen carefully. Okay?" she said, her voice was shaky as she tried to maintain her composure. She was still having tears in her eyes.

"What...?"

"Please, don't ever try to talk to me, henceforth. I still have respect for you as I can't forget what you have done for me. So, stop hounding me, it's disturbing me."

"Aditi..."

"Please understand, Keshav. Now, we as a pair have already become infamous for no reason in college. If anybody sees us talking or roaming together in college again, the issue will be hyped," she said, almost pleading with tears in her eyes.

I took one last look at her – her beautiful but angry, wet and sad face – and turned around.

I heard the sound of her footsteps get fainter as she walked away.

I could feel tears in my eyes. I was feeling lonely. I went in the lawn and sat on a bench, all alone.

After a few minutes, I returned to the hostel. That day, the same college, which I had loved a lot, felt like a graveyard. There was silence everywhere, except for the sound of the vehicles crossing the hostel building.

My heartbeat stopped, thinking of her. She was going away from me. I burst into tears. She had stolen my spirit; an injury no other person could see.

I kept on crying loudly and cried myself to sleep. I woke up hearing the voices of my hostel mates, asking me to come down for dinner.

"Is everything fine?" Vivaan asked me while I had my dinner. I nodded, saying all was well. But he had more questions, "You were not seen today."

"Yes, I was not feeling well," I replied.

Vivaan did not ask anything more, but his silence had many questions, for which I did not have answers.

17

When nothing goes right

She had stopped talking and had muted my whole life. I lost interest in friends, life or family.

My mind was thinking about her.

I knew what I was going through, but I didn't want to share it with my friends.

I wasn't sure what I should do. If I forced her, maybe I'd hurt her more, or should I leave it to time and wait for her to come back to me. I was in a dilemma.

After that conversation, she refused to take my calls. She didn't reply to any of my messages.

I waited for her at the college entrance every morning. She came, ignored me and went in quickly.

Nothing was working out for me anymore. Everything that has a beginning has an end too. My perception of life changed after this.

How life changed in the blink of an eye!

For the last few days, I used to go to college and sat outside the classroom, watching her. She did not even bother to look at me. She was behaving differently; she was not looking at me and she had stopped smiling.

I had already missed ten days' classes by then.

Soon I realized I had lost her forever. I had lost her smile. I had lost her friendship. I had lost her voice. But still, somewhere in my heart, I believed she was sad in her heart and angry with me for the time being, and some day she would come back in my life.

Three months passed away and I had hardly attended the classes.

I was broken and kept to myself.

Several times, I thought of visiting her at her house and clear everything to her and her parents from my side, but couldn't gather the courage to do so. Perhaps I was afraid of worsening things.

I was sitting alone when Vivaan came to the terrace, "Hey Keshav, what are you doing alone here?" he asked me and sat next to me.

I smiled at him casually, and kept looking at the empty road.

"Exam dates are out. Third and last sessional are starting from next week followed by end semester exams. Are you prepared?" Vivaan asked me.

I gave a sly smile and kept staring at the road.

"Okay, I am going to my room. I need to study," he informed me and left, while I kept sitting there. I was not even aware of my subjects of the seventh semester, but I was not concerned about it. I was only concerned about Aditi.

I kept walking around the hostel all alone. I pushed myself into my room and kept my door closed, as if I could trap the memories inside. Though my hostel mates tried to be there for me, the truth was that I was all alone.

"Why don't you prepare for the sessional?" Reyansh asked me, concerned. I didn't reply.

"I am speaking to you, Keshav. That girl has spoiled your life. Forget her, think about your career."

I looked at him and smiled.

"You will gain nothing by doing this. You are wasting your own life and time," he tried to convince me.

I remained silent.

"Keshav, three months have passed, it's November now. Friend, come out of this, I care for you," he reiterated, showing concern.

I stood up, and went out saying, "Sorry for disturbing you friend; you study. I will waste my time downstairs."

"Wait Keshav, listen to me ...." He shouted from behind, but I didn't stop.

After all, I also missed third mid-terms sessionals in seventh semester.

Final exams came. I hadn't studied at all. I was going to screw up everything. I already had. I was making my life hell. I was not able to concentrate on anything. I had stopped listening to others.

Exams came and went.

Somehow I appeared in all the exams and wrote whatever I could.

In semester break, I didn't go home this time and stayed back in the hostel.

By now, in January, our final eighth-semester had already started. It was the time for campus placements. All the students were excited for the job selection process that they were going to go through before graduating in engineering.

Several multinational companies visited our college by the start of January. I also faced campus placement of various ECE and IT companies, but couldn't get selected in any of them, due to my state of mind. I was depressed.

So, I couldn't even fight for the upcoming selection in companies. Now, after my rejection in campus placement, I was even more concerned regarding my job opportunities. What would I say to my parents?

18

Trying to console myself

After my half-break-up, with Aditi, and rejection in campus placement, I tried to console myself. I didn't inform my parents about my bad performance in campus placement. My personality had changed. Now, I started attending every class and was always busy in making notes. I had stopped looking at Aditi in class. I would sit with my friends in the hostels, but didn't contribute to the conversation. Initially, they tried to cheer me up. They tried everything to help me get over Aditi.

However, their efforts didn't work for me.

After attending a few classes in the final semester, suddenly, Aditi stopped coming to the college. I thought there would be some family function at her home or else she might be ill. I enquired with her friends, but they also didn't know about Aditi's absence. I waited for ten days, but she didn't come to the college at all.

Further, in the month of February, preparations for Engifest had already started all around in DTU.

One afternoon, I was sitting outside in the main lawn. Vivaan came to me and asked, "Have you heard about Aditi?"

"No, what happened?" I asked eagerly.

"She has decided to leave the college after the fest. She will perform in a few events in the fest and after that she will not come," Vivaan broke out.

"How do you know all this?" I asked.

"Her friends are telling, they were completing the migration formalities for Aditi in admin block," he said.

I was stunned to know this. What would have happened? I thought.

19

Wavering emotions

17 February 2015

I had to talk to Aditi. I decided to do it during the Engifest. Aditi had already won the music competition in the solo vocals category. She was also taking part in choreography. I took my place in the audience early, sitting in the front row.

Aditi performed on stage with incredible grace. The crowd burst into applause as she did a perfect cartwheel.

In the last act, Aditi took the mic and sang a song. Her clear and tuneful voice earned a round of spontaneous applause.

The show ended and the crowd cheered.

I slipped out and then sprinted into the green room.

I knocked on the door.

A girl student peeked out.

"What?"

"I need to talk to someone."

"Sorry, only girls allowed inside."

"Is Aditi there?"

"She is changing, wait."

I had little choice. I sat on a ledge opposite the classroom. I waited for a long time.

Forty minutes later, Aditi stepped out.

Deliberately, she took brisk steps away from me.

"Aditi…," I said.

She stopped. However, she didn't turn towards me. Her hands froze, as if uncomfortable.

"Please…," I said.

She turned toward me.

"Hi, Keshav."

I stood squarely in front of her.

"I want to talk. Give me five minutes," I said.

"Anything important?"

"To me, it is."

"I'm listening, tell me."

We stood in a dark corridor, facing each other stiffly. It didn't seem like the right place to talk.

I saw her face. She was still the most beautiful girl in the world to me.

"Not here. Somewhere else?"

"Oh, really?" she said.

"Sorry, I didn't mean that. Somewhere that is lit and we can sit."

"The café sounds okay?" she said.

"Yes, cafe is fine."

We walked to the cafe. As expected, it was packed with DTU crowd.

"It is crowded. Is it okay if we talk in the lawn?" she said.

I looked at her. She seemed to have calmed down a little.

"Yeah, okay."

We went to the same college lawn in which we had spent hundreds of hours together.

"So…?" Aditi said.

"You were really great on stage and congrats on winning the solo music competition!"

"Oh, thank you. That's nice of you, Keshav."

"Amazing show," I said, clearing my throat and gathering some courage.

"Thanks. Is that all you wanted to say to me?"

"I'm really sorry."

"Have heard it a hundred times in the past four months."

"Please Aditi, forgive me."

"I have forgiven you. I have also moved on. It's all in the past. It's over, there is no issue. In fact, I have learnt to live without you. I unknowingly had depended on you."

"Aditi, I think, one never leaves a true friendship for a few faults. Nobody is perfect, nobody is correct. And in the end, affection is always greater than perfection."

"So, that's it?"

I looked into her eyes. In the dim light, I could not spot any emotion on her face. I felt weak in her presence. I tried to fight back my tears.

"I want us to be friends again," I said.

"Why?" she said, her voice as cold as the winter night.

Did she miss nothing about me? I wanted to scream at the top of my voice. Of course, I couldn't.

She left me speechless.

However, suddenly, she took my hand in her. Her soft fingers pressed into my wrist, making me a little comfortable.

"Listen, Keshav," she said. "I am sorry, I am being this way, cold and aloof."

Her warm touch melted my resolve to keep my composure. I loved her touch. I didn't know if I could hold back my tears anymore.

"Please give me a second chance to prove myself," I said, almost pleading.

"Keshav, I'm not angry with you anymore. I have high regard for you in my heart. I'm still your friend. Don't break your heart.

But, it is anyway not possible for us to be so close again. I have to move forward in life, leaving all these relations behind."

"Thanks for still considering me as your friend. But, why can't we be close again like before?"

"Because, I am leaving."

"What…?"

"Yes, I'm leaving the college."

"What? Like quitting B. Tech?"

She nodded in agreement.

"Actually, I'm dropping out."

"You're in the last year. You won't finish your degree?"

"You all know Keshav, I have never cared much for formal education. You know engineering has always been a second preference for me."

I looked at her, shocked.

"But, why?"

She shrugged.

"Aditi, you're dropping out from the prestigious B. Tech in DTU. There must be a strong reason," I said.

Our eyes met. Maybe it was my imagination, but for a moment, I felt the same connection to her as I had in the past.

"Keshav, please."

"Yeah, fine. Anyway, are you still thinking about quitting or is it final?"

"Pretty final."

"Why?"

She took a deep breath.

"Actually, it's due to my passion of becoming a singing star. I have got a golden opportunity in Mumbai to fulfil my dreams of becoming a national level singer. I have got selected through a competition among five most talented singers from all over India; these five singers shall be given extensive training for six months in Geetmala Music Academy. My training would start from 24th February, the next week. So, I have to reach Mumbai the day after tomorrow."

"What…?" I said.

"It happened so fast, and I have convinced my parents and family. Now, they are happily ready to allow me to drop B. Tech and immediately go to Mumbai. Especially, my father had decided to support her daughter in achieving her dreams," Aditi said.

I remained quiet. Shock waves ran through me.

I smirked and turned to her.

"That's life, it happens sometimes," she further said.

"Have you gone mad, Aditi?"

"You've lost the right to talk to me like that after that hostel incident," she said.

"Oh, I'm sorry."

"It's fine. Keshav, it is my choice to go to Mumbai. Nobody is forcing me. I want to leave."

"You could finish your degree. Go to Mumbai later for singing training. Why only now?"

"I want to achieve my dreams as fast as possible and this music academy in Mumbai promises me all that."

"Are you sure?"

"Yeah," she said.

"Aditi, nobody drops out of engineering college like this."

"Oh, come on, Keshav. Most Indians need a degree to get a job and make a living. I don't need that. I don't have to do a job, and you know that, right?"

She wasn't wrong. Losers like me need to study, else we have no future. People who are born at 108, New Friends Colony, Delhi could do whatever they want in life.

"You want to say something more?" she asked.

"What do I say? Surprised. Shocked. I don't know."

"People normally say Congratulations."

'Yeah," I said, but didn't congratulate her.

"I hope we can move on in our respective lives forgetting whatever has happened. Right?"

I nodded.

"Are you sure you're doing the right thing?" I managed to say one more time.

"I'm following my heart. That's usually doing the right thing, right?"

"I don't know. Sometimes following your heart leads you nowhere."

"I am sorry, Keshav, if I hurt you."

I was not able to utter a single word. There was a pin drop silence between us.

"Goodbye," she said, looking at my face.

"Goodbye, Aditi," I said.

It was hard to hold back my tears. I wanted her to leave, now.

"Take care then," she said and came forward for a usual goodbye hug.

I stepped back.

I didn't want any more fake hugs from her.

She understood my hesitation and withdrew with grace. She smiled at me one last time and slid into her car.

I sat down on the grass. I cried. The desolate campus roads meant nobody could see me. Months of pain condensed into tears.

After a while, I collected everything from the lawn and stood up and went to my room.

20

The worst days of my life

So, it was true. Aditi was out of my life. Why did it have to end like this? I really didn't deserve this. I could never forget the days we had spent together. We had a lot of fun, especially when we were together. I would always remember her presence in college. The laughter that we shared, the dreams that we had, and the promises we made. But those dreams changed with time and left a big hole in my heart.

I knew she had moved on in her life to achieve her dreams. But I still wished she cared for me.

I had spent the most beautiful moments with her. That was why her outright rejection made me lose hopes in everything.

I was all alone in college. I missed her everywhere. I stopped going to the college cafeteria. I wanted to avoid everyone. Everything seemed to be different. I was missing her badly. Viavaan, Reyansh and Chirag would come to see me. I had been ignoring them for the last few days. I was not in the mood to face the world.

When you really love someone from the bottom of your heart and she rejects you, it is often difficult to move on.

Love is so strange – sometimes it gives you the reason to live and sometimes the reason to leave life. Day after day, time passed away. I cut off all contacts with her, blocked her on social media and changed my number too.

It made me feel better, like she did not exist anymore.

But I had no clue what was happening to me, I was shattered completely… broken and depressed!

Doing all this was necessary in order to forget her completely. Though it hurt, I had no other choice left with me.

21

Shattered dreams

My lifestyle had changed, and so had my behaviour. I had almost stopped attending college. Meanwhile, the result of the seventh semester came out. I had flunked in three subjects and my attendance was low.

"I think you all are not interested in doing engineering anymore. Now, do one thing. Call your parents within a few days. And Keshav, I am very disappointed to see you getting three backs. Such a brilliant student, a DTU topper; what has gone wrong to you my son?" the Head of Department warned me in particular. I was shocked to see my results. What can be worse than this? First you land up doing engineering, work hard, become a topper, and then you get your love. Later you lose your love, get rejected in campus placements, and now get such a bad semester result in B.Tech.

Everyone was going away. I needed someone who could take care of me. I would be screwed if I showed this result to my parents. My life was at a standstill. She never once looked back, even though I was still waiting for her.

My heart said she would come back to me one day.

But for now, all my dreams and expectations were buried in the sand.

I had a dream of becoming an author of repute and earning a lot of money for my parents. Now that dream couldn't be realized.

I wanted my parents to be happy by getting selected in a public sector or government job. That dream had vanished too.

No son wants his parents to cry in front of him just because of a girl. But I could not forget her. I was guilty of deceiving my parents. All my dreams were shattered.

I told Vivaan about the result. He was shocked and disappointed.

I tried telling the result at home. But I was not able to.

I didn't have the courage to face my parents.

22

A broken guy

I was completely broken. I wasn't even able to believe myself. I was devastated and frustrated on my wrong decisions and felt helpless on the overall current situation. Nothing was working for me. I was miles away from peace. Anxiety, guilt and fear were now overtaking my mind. How could I be calm?

My life had changed completely. Nothing seemed to be working out for me anymore. I had lost everything in life.

It was late evening, and the sun was turning red, all set to melt into the horizon. The birds had started to return to their nests. I was sitting in my room while my other friends were busy in their respective rooms preparing for the final year mid-terms. There was a heavy silence in my room; the only sound was of the insects.

A long ring on my phone broke my trance. I pulled it out to check it. It was my dad. I couldn't pick it. What would I say to him? How would I convey my results to him? How would I convey my debacles in campus placement to him? What was I going to do? I didn't have an answer.

Life is so difficult to live, so painful to survive and so bitter to know about, and now I feel alone. I miss my memories, I said to myself and started crying.

I closed my eyes, took a deep breath and sat down in desperation.

My phone started ringing again. My dad was waiting for me to talk. I tried to control myself and took his call.

"Hello! Where are you?" my dad asked, straightway.

I didn't have an answer.

"Why were you not picking up my call?" I could feel the tension in his voice.

A drop of tear rolled down my right eye.

"Are you crying? Tell me," he insisted, worried.

I don't know what divine connection our parents have with us. We stay thousands of miles away, still they can feel our pain. Words are not the only medium for communication with parents.

"I am okay," I lied in a shattered voice.

"Are you alone and sad?" he asked softly.

"I am okay Papa," I repeated.

"Come back home. I am booking the next flight to Lucknow. Don't worry for anything," he assured me.

I broke down. I started to cry just like anything over the phone. I just wanted to hug my dad that very moment. I needed him.

"No degree made in this world tells you about the abilities of a child. If at all, it tells you about a few numbers in various subjects and that too will be forgotten, sooner or later. I don't want you to be a broken man due to failure in engineering. I want you to be a great learner. An engineering degree is someone else's way of telling you who you are. But, always remember Keshav, you're the creator of your own life. I have cherished all your success. I love you for them. Don't you remember how happy I was whenever you topped your class? I love you with all your failures now. Don't feel bad! I am proud of being your father and will always be," Papa tried to convince me in an emotional tone.

"Keshav beta, everyone's life starts and ends with open hands, but it depends upon you how much you achieve in your life and show it to the world during the journey of your life. In fact, your thoughts define how you live, so just live your life the way you want. I have no point to demotivate you, my son," Papa continued.

"Life is a journey and we are the travellers. Many ups and downs come during this journey. We have to face them patiently, and one day, we definitely get successful. Life doesn't end if you get failure in your exams, placement or relationship, but yeah, you get hurt so much that you don't believe that there is any other reason to live. But look closely in your life, you will definitely see one. We are alive, that means we can try anything multiple times; practice makes a man perfect, so never lose hope in life. Life is precious, don't spoil it if a small misfortune happens to you," Papa further continued.

"I love you, Papa." I cried like a baby.

"Come back home. Right now, I am out of station and will be there tomorrow morning. I promise."

"Yes, Papa."

The day I had received that phone call from my father, I had been a broken guy. I had lost all faith in myself.

23

Should I live more?

So, I went home the next day, according to my dad's advice. Dad also reached home from his outstation work. My parents and Garima were stunned to see my mental and physical condition. I could not hold my tears anymore in front of them. I told my parents about everything that had happened to me. I told them about Aditi, my dismal academic results and my placement failures in college. They seemed extremely worried. However, my parents consoled me in every possible way and made me understand that failure was a part of life. Dad advised me to take rest at home for some time and not to think about exams and other stuff. However, I could not convince myself. I was crying in my heart for the way things had gone wrong for me during the last eight months. I started to curse myself that I couldn't fulfill my parents' dreams. I was a proud DTU topper, and now, I couldn't even pass the exams. I could only regret my decisions now. Even then, I could not forget Aditi. I could never get that image out of my head.

On that night at home, I couldn't sleep. My parents and sister took extreme care of me. They did every possible thing to bring me out of my depression. My mom would pass most of the time with me. But, my mind was not ready to accept anything.

I woke up one morning, feeling afraid. It was a kind of fear that I had never experienced in my life. It was an unusual feeling in my stomach which was spreading upwards slowly. After sometime, I felt like somebody was squeezing my throat tightly. I felt nervous and extremely scared. I started walking around in my room.

I walked to my window and looked down. It was like any other day – an ordinary day for everybody; but for me, it wasn't.

I was terrified, the fear started gripping me. There were no words to express the fear and pain. My heart was beating so fast that I could hear my heartbeats. I felt a cold sweat on my chest. It was irrational, strange and terrifying. I tried to speak but was drowned in the massive panic that hit me. I closed my eyes. I tried to calm myself in every possible way.

It's okay; take it easy, I kept repeating to myself. But the words seemed to have no effect. Soon, I felt pain in my body and could barely breathe.

I did not understand what was happening to me. All I knew was that I was too scared. I had never experienced this kind of restlessness in my life.

Finally, I collected my strength and walked to the kitchen.

I saw my dad making a cup of coffee. By now, I could barely breathe.

My face was ashen. My hands were cold.

"Papa," I called out in a slow voice.

My voice could hardly be heard. My dad looked at me in great surprise with his eyes wide open. He immediately realized that there was something wrong with me.

"Beta, what's the matter?" he rushed toward me.

He sounded anxious, tense.

I burst into uncontrollable tears. By now, my mom and Garima also came into the kitchen. They started crying, seeing me in that state.

My dad held me. "What happened, what happened....?" he kept repeating.

I had no idea what happened. I could not explain my condition.

My mother held my head and kept it on her lap.

"I am scared, dad," my voice seemed to belong to somebody else.

"Calm down; whatever it is, we will sort it out," he said.

His words had no effect on my brain.

"Is there something wrong with your health?" mom asked.

"Mom, I'm nervous and so scared of something unknown," I said.

The fear was rising by the minute. I was in a state of panic by now.

"I am scared, mom, very scared," I muttered, sounding like a lost child.

My emotions were spiralling out of control. It seemed I was still sobbing internally.

"What are you scared of? Can you tell me?" asked my mother.

I could not speak.

My parents did not know what to do. But they understood that all those recent unexpected failures were having a serious impact on me. They took me to the living room and made me sit on the sofa. My mother got me a glass of cold water.

"Drink this," she said.

I obeyed. I was breathing fast.

"May be it is just taking time for you to forget everything. Beta, you don't worry at all, we are with you. First you recover from this mental state and then we will collectively take a decision for your career; whatever you want," said my dad.

I did not know what to say, my hands had now turned icy. I did not want to hear anything. From some place far away, I could hear my mother's voice asking me if I felt better.

I could not respond at all.

I closed my eyes; I felt my dad's hand on my back. He was rubbing my back, trying to calm me. He was saying, "There is nothing to be afraid of. I am here now. Don't worry. I am here," he kept repeating it and he kept rubbing my back.

"Take deep breaths," he said.

I did.

"In and out. Inhale and exhale," he kept repeating.

I breathed just as he had told me and gradually the panic subsided. I began to feel a little better. I opened my eyes.

I saw my mother's and Garima's worried faces. I could see that my dad was worried too, but he was trying to hide it.

I felt better now. There was no fear or panic anymore. I was still not completely calm, but it was not uncontrollable now. I could think and focus.

Everyone could see it on my face.

"What happened?" asked my mom.

Her voice was a bit unsteady.

"I don't know, mom," I answered.

"Are you still thinking about those things?" she asked. She knew it was a panic attack or an anxiety attack.

I didn't speak.

The fear was gone, but it was replaced by a depressing feeling which made my heart sink.

"You take rest today as well. You will feel better tomorrow," said my dad.

I told dad I did not want to go to DTU anymore. My mother looked anxious. She wanted me to assure her that I was fine.

I spent the rest of the day in my room. Just lying on my bed. My parents were sitting beside me.

A few more days passed, at home.

I was still not feeling well.

It was the first time I realized that there was perhaps something very wrong with my health.

I had tried to fool myself and my parents, assuring them that I was fine. I thought I would be very strong and shake it off. I tried my best to force myself. But things only got worse.

My father called up the college and spoke to the Dean. I felt a void around me. I felt like I was dead from inside. I had been experiencing a deep sense of pain. I was not interested in anything – social media, messages, books or phone. I just wanted to lie in my bed and go deeper into the vacuum in my mind. I tried to continue writing my book, but no words came.

No thoughts came.

It was a horrible place to be trapped in. I did not want to be there. But there seemed to be no escape.

I felt down and depressed. I didn't know what was happening to me and why I was feeling that kind of stress and fear. I tried to make these thoughts go away, but all in vain. I didn't want to do this engineering anymore. I convinced myself. There was nothing to look forward to.

I picked up a pen and tried to write in my diary what I was feeling at that time, but words too seemed to have abandoned me. The pen refused to move. I was unable to read and write too.

With no improvement in my mental condition, my parents did everything for me, whatever they could. They arranged a meeting with a well-known psychiatrist, Dr Neeraj Pandey. My parents considered it fortunate that he had agreed to examine me. I was quiet and refused to speak to either of my parents.

Dr Neeraj Pandey did not even speak to me and merely wrote out a prescription with more medication.

April 2015

I had lost everything during the last few months – my friends, my studies, my happiness and even my parents' trust. I had caused my family so much pain. But, even after all this, would she come back into my life, I was not sure.

I felt a mounting sense of despair about the stress and strain I was putting my parents. I thought that I was a burden not only on my parents, but also on my own self. This was frightening for me; a world of darkness and avoid. I got progressively worse.

I didn't want to be a liability anymore. I wanted to stop it.

My existence was completely pointless now. There was only one way out of this mess and that was to end my life.

It was after four more days of misery, hopelessness and extreme agony that I finally gathered enough courage and attempted to finish myself.

It was around eleven in the night when I started to creep out very quietly.

My hands were trembling and my feet were shaking as I tried my best to balance myself. After many failed attempts, somehow, I managed to open the door to the terrace.

As I reached the terrace, the cold breeze hit me. I took in a deep breath. I looked at the sky with the million of twinkling stars. I went to the edge of the wall and looked down. The hard concrete pavement below stared at me, as if daring me to jump. I peered a little further, and walked along the edge of the wall, choosing a spot to jump. The night was very silent. I climbed on the wall of the terrace and sat looking down, gathering courage in my heart to jump.

"Keshav! Oh my god, what are you doing here?" Suddenly my dad's voice cut through my thoughts and the next moment I turned around and saw my dad rushing towards me.

My dad was shocked. He had woken up with an uneasy feeling that night, and when he came to my room, he found me missing. Somehow, dad had come up to the terrace to look for me.

I did not know what to say to my dad. But I was sure that he had understood my intentions perfectly, looking at my passive face and crumpled, defeated shoulders.

I had never seen my dad cry and dejected, but that night I saw the tears of defeat and agony that he blinked back. I saw the sheer helplessness and anger at being able to do nothing for me on his face. He was such a strong man. He had always given us the best of everything.

But that night, I saw him broken and sad and it was because of me. He was shattered. He did not say anything to me. He did not shout at me either. He took my hands in a firm grip and quietly led me down the stairs. "Sorry Papa," I managed to say.

24

Psychiatric hospital

I was waiting for my turn outside the office of Dr Vikram Awasthi in a famous psychiatric hospital in Delhi – Pragyan Institute of Mental Health & Behavioural Sciences. My parents were inside with the doctor, while I was waiting outside. I was relentlessly tapping my feet, trying to dry my sweaty palms. Anxiety overwhelmed me during each of these visits to different doctors in Gorakhpur and Lucknow in recent times.

My sister, too, had come along. I looked around the sitting area of patients in the hall. There were at least a hundred patients and their relatives. How was it possible that so many people had mental health problems? How could so many people need help like this?

Were they also depressed like me?

What issues did they have?

I wondered if there was any engineering college dropout like me. I doubted it.

In the hall, I also saw a poster with the title *Love Yourself*. I felt a connection with every sentence in the poster that described the importance of nurturing relationship between one's soul and one's physical body.

Behind the closed chamber, the doctor asked my parents multiple questions about their son's recent behaviour. He thoroughly read my file that had the findings and opinions of several other doctors. “Keshav repeatedly insists that he doesn’t want to live anymore. He says he has no interest left in life. His appetite has steadily decreased and he is losing weight,” said my mother, her voice cracking.

My father held her hand tightly.

“I need to talk to him. We should put him on stronger medication,” the doctor said as he started writing some prescription.

“He is sitting outside, doctor,” my father said.

“Call him in,” the doctor said as he turned on his recording device.

My mother came out and saw me sitting impatiently, rubbing my palms together.

She came to me. “Keshav, the doctor is calling you.”

“Mom, I have faced so many doctors back home. Now, I don’t want to answer the same stupid questions here yet again,” I replied, agitated.

“It will be fine, Keshav. He just wants to speak to you,” she lightly squeezed my shoulder.

“Oh yeah, I know It will be all right the way you always claim it’ll be, and then I won’t remember anything the next morning,” I said, annoyed.

“Please, Keshav. Come for us. It is for your betterment,” she said, her eyes pleading.

I faked a half-smile and went into the room with her. It was a spacious room with several medical instruments on a table in one corner of the room.

“Hello, Keshav! How are you?” The doctor asked, placing my case file aside as he rose to shake his hand.

Dr Vikram Awasthi was a corpulent man in his mid-sixties who had been practicing psychiatry for forty years. According to him, I was probably suffering from depression, anxiety and stress and the only cure for that was strong medication and psychotherapy.

"I'm fine, as always," I said, trying to be cordial.

The doctor started asking questions. I felt trapped, concerned, exasperated and suddenly very tired. The doctor asked me every question and was also recording my responses. He was writing down everything I was saying.

Initially, I answered all the questions with great solemnity. The more I talked, the more evident was my sadness. I also told the doctor how I was feeling insecure and afraid in life.

"How do you feel all of a sudden?" Doctor asked another question to help me open up a bit further.

After a long pause, I began to cautiously describe my rapid mood swings. I also described my roller coaster emotions, which had begun after I'd left college. Sometimes in nights, I would have periods of intense loneliness and depression.

"How was last night?" the doctor asked.

"I don't know what happened to me last night," I said, taking my eyes away from doctor.

"I have heard you had a tough time at your placement interviews at campus," the doctor finally started probing deeper.

"Oh, yeah," I tried to look calm and composed.

I interlaced my fingers and started tapping my feet on the floor again.

"It seems you don't want to talk about it?"

"What nonsense are you talking about, doctor? I don't want to speak to you. I want to leave."

I stood up, abruptly. My father asked me to sit down, but I pushed his hand away and walked out of the room.

"I am really scared, doctor," my mother pleaded.

"Mrs Dixit, his case is very different. I think he is suffering from a stress disorder," said the doctor.

"What is that?" my mother was hearing this new diagnosis for the first time.

"He was fine and completely normal when he came to Gorakhpur for Diwali holidays. But, after that due to those sudden unfortunate incidents, he is behaving like this, otherwise, he excelled academically throughout in life," she said.

"This happens sometimes, Mrs Dixit. Patients generally bury themselves in a task or goal and become obsessed with it. He probably suppressed his emotions after the incident."

It was after thirty minutes that my parents emerged from the doctor's room. Their faces were quite grim.

"Keshav, Dr Vikram Awasthi has studied your case in detail. He strongly feels that it is best that you are admitted and kept under observation here in the hospital," said my dad, as he put his hand on my shoulder.

It sounded like a death sentence. I was in a complete shock. I did not want to come here at all and now they were going to admit and keep me here. It was so unacceptable to me. But they were not giving me any choice.

I could not speak, even though I wanted to scream.

"We have opted for a private room for you. It is the best they have. You will get better very soon," my dad continued.

"Please dad, take me back home. I promise I will not do anything like that again," I pleaded. The fear of being admitted in a psychiatric hospital made me feel hopeless. "Please dad, please don't leave me here. I want to go back home," I cried again.

"Doctor has recommended a trial run of antidepressants, which he said would hopefully help control your manic symptoms and normalize your sleeping, behavioral and thought patterns.

He assured us that in a few days, you would recover and become normal again."

"But, dad, I don't want to stay in a psychiatric hospital, please take me home," I pleaded.

"Look, this is not easy for us. This is for your betterment. How long can we see you in pain? You were not getting any better, beta. You will be looked after well here," he said with finality in his voice.

I closed my eyes and tried to calm my pounding heartbeats. I desperately looked around my surroundings.

I was brought into the private room. The room was just like any normal hospital room. I did not want myself in the ward of a psychiatric hospital, relegated as a patient, a highly disturbed one at that, needing high observation and care.

My parents and sister too stayed there in a nearby hotel.

Our various relatives also came to see me. I stayed there for seven days and got treatment under intensive observation of some senior doctors.

It was indeed a special kind of experience and I felt gradual improvement in my mental state and health. I got a positive vibe towards life.

I felt relaxed in my heart. I got rid of pain and fear. I could breathe easily now.

I could sense things around myself with ease and could talk to my parents as I used to earlier. The darkness disappeared from my surroundings now.

After the treatment, I got discharge and we went to see my uncle in Noida. My uncle had helped us a lot when I was in the hospital. He was a spiritual and religious person. We spent fifteen days in a spiritual and religious centre on the outskirts of Noida. Luckily, the centre was devoted to Lord Narayana. I attended all the spiritual and religious sessions at the centre. Besides regular sessions, often in the evening, I would sit, for hours, in front of the beautiful large statue of Lord Laxmi Narayana installed in the centre of the temple. I would mediate and tried to talk to my heart and soul.

After spending fifteen days in the lap of Lord Vishnu, I got some self-realization. Some positive energy flowed into my body. It felt like I had found new hope to live for. My smile was back on my face. By now, my goals, my dreams of life were visible to me. Now, I had a positive approach towards my life.

During my meditation, I felt as if Lord Vishnu was talking to me, "Son, every situation in life is temporary. So, when life is good, make sure you enjoy it fully. And when life is not so good, remember that it will not last forever and better days are on their way. Many ups and downs come during the journey of life. We have to face them patiently and one day we definitely get successful."

I remained silent.

Tears were rolling down my face.

I collected myself and promised to Lord Vishnu, "Lord, my body felt like a cage, and you have unlocked me with your words. You have opened a door I didn't know was there. You took out the pain from me and made me bear it by still seeing the person inside me. And for that reason alone, I feel I will be a bird in the sky again, able to sing once more."

Lord Vishnu smiled and gestured, "Keshav, prove yourself in the battle of life, love yourself, and achieve your dreams, get enormous success in life and show the world that you can do it."

"My Lord, I promise you, from now onwards, my goal will be to achieve my dreams with a firm approach," I replied, wiping my tears.

Soon, I opened my eyes, came out of my meditation and realized a unique energy inside my body and soul.

I thanked Lord Vishnu again and again for his motivation.

Now, it was my turn to prove myself.

I needed to plan my career path and show everyone that Keshav Dixit was still alive.

25

Starting a new life

May 2015

I returned home and the first thing I did was to groom myself. I could see a new energetic Keshav coming out.

I sat down on my bed and started thinking on how to move forward in life now?? What should I do now? I had already dropped out of B. Tech, so a job was out of the question.

Then, what next? I kept on thinking and thinking for hours.

I thought of taking full control over my life. Failure had taught me things that I never knew about myself. Actually, failure made me discover my true self. It gave me an inner security which did not come from passing university examinations. I realized that I had a strong will and discipline, which were also classic strengths of an introvert.

After a lot of thinking, I decided to go with my passion to write fiction books and become an author. I had so many stories to tell to the world since school days.

However, I had no clue of how to begin writing books. I pulled out my all old journals of stories which I had written earlier and started to read them to recollect all those stories. This was the easiest way to start writing some new books.

My mother entered the room and seeing me busy with old books, was overcome with happiness. She thought of asking me about it, but didn't want to disrupt my thought process. She just looked at me from afar with satisfaction on her face and left.

Now, I could not cry all my life. I had to find a way to move on. I wanted to prove to everyone that I wasn't a loser. I couldn't fool myself and spoil my life. I wanted to achieve something.

Enthusiasm did shine through my gleaming face and sparkling eyes.

I was back to my old self again. I enjoyed the music I was listening to without analyzing the lyrics.

I was excited to write.

26

My struggle to craft my life again

June 2015

Although I had written various stories and won many awards in essay competitions in school days, a saleable novel was totally new and confusing for me. I had so many fiction stories in my mind, but didn't know how to start writing a book or novel. I browsed the internet and searched advice from experts and also some video lectures to know how to start writing a bestseller. I spent almost two days surfing the internet to find some clues for writing. I also read few online self-help books that claimed to make an author out of anyone. Those books and video lectures gave a standard three-act structure to follow – introduce the character; build conflict in story; resolve conflict. I collected my thoughts and start writing an inspirational fiction novel in parts. Initially, I faced difficulty in framing plots, but experts' video lectures advised that an author should have an overactive imagination, good enough for amusing people and at the same time must be able to create a fantasy world for readers. So, after long self-study, I absorbed myself day and night in writing my first novel. My parents were somewhat relieved to see me work that way.

Dad told me, "Beta, you choose for yourself what you want in your life, now. Live life the way you want; live the life of your dreams. We'll never force our ambition on you."

I started writing the manuscript. I burnt the candles at both ends for three months to write my first book. It was a motivational love story, inspired form my own story. So, I completed it in minimum time.

After completing the manuscript of the book, the next most important thing was to publish it with some reputed publisher. So, I went to various websites and found that most of eminent publishers initially invite only few chapters of the manuscript, not the full story. I extracted the best three chapters and also wrote the synopsis of the book and author details. I sent these three documents along with the covering letter to most of the leading publishers of India. I was confident of my story and manuscript.

After sending my sample manuscript and synopsis to various publishers, I became workless. I didn't have any writing work now. Nevertheless, I started working with another story and began writing my second book.

So, as time passed, I received the response of a publisher for my manuscript:

Dear Mr Keshav Dixit,

We really appreciate getting a chance to consider your book proposal. However, we regret to say that we won't be able to take it up for publication. We hope you find a suitable publisher for your book and our best wishes for its success!

My manuscript had been rejected straight away. I felt a stab of disappointment.

What went wrong? I was thinking. I didn't expect such kind of response from the publishers.

In the next few days, my manuscript was rejected one after another, by fourteen publishers. Were they not able to judge the story of the book? That meant the story didn't matter for most of the publishers. Did these publishers publish books of only well-established and best-selling authors? Now, what should I do to get my book published? Engulfed in thoughts, I went to the terrace. I gazed upwards, but could not see any stars. I thought that no matter what I was doing, it just seemed like things were not working for me. This was a frustrating reality.

As the time passed, my struggle continued. I talked to few publishers on phone, but, no publisher was ready to publish my book. One publisher told me that there was no market for first-time authors. No publisher could invest and risk money with first-time authors. For me, it was very easy to give up at that juncture. I had not had any success in the recent past. It seemed as if my life was jinxed. But, this time, I decided not to give up, rather persist in odd situations.

So, I again searched the internet and found so many options; one among them was to publish book through self-publishing mode, but for that, publishers were charging a hefty publishing fee. I was totally confused, how to move further and publish my book.

I came to know that famous authors don't need to seek an agent and publishers; rather, publishers come to them to publish their books. They don't have to worry if their books will sell or not. Famous authors don't have day jobs and have the privilege of doing only what they love – write.

Most of the famous authors came to success through failure. I wanted to become one of them. So, after reading this, one thing was clear to me that now I wouldn't surrender to circumstances. I never felt dejected enough to give it up, though. I was determined in my mind to publish my work.

I sat down and started thinking what were the ways left for me to publish the book, now. After extensive research I thought of self-publishing my book. For that I searched for some local small-scale vendors for typesetting and composing work. However, the total cost of all vendors was on the higher side. I said to myself, "If I adopt this model then, the cost of my book would be too high and who would purchase a highly priced book of a first-time author."

Luckily, one day I found a vendor who would prepare and publish conference proceedings, journals, etc., for college and other institutions on contract basis. I had a detailed meeting with that vendor. I found that the publication cost suited me. So, I signed an agreement with the vendor and ordered the publication of one thousand copies.

The vendor took fifteen days to make my book ready. When I saw the beautiful book, I was jubilant as it was my first novel. My parents were also happy to see the book in printed form.

Next, I registered as a seller on the e-market places. I also self-published my e-book on Amazon Kindle without any cost. So, now my book was present to the readers on online marketplaces and bookstores. At the same time, I realized that marketing was an essential part of book promotion. Now, since I was both the author and the seller of my book, so I had to promote my book through various channels. For that, first I set up a small studio in my house and prepared a promotional video for my book. I uploaded my video on YouTube. In addition to this, I also uploaded my promotional video on other social media. On some selected websites, I promoted my book and wrote blogs related to the book to attract readers. From teasers on YouTube to Facebook marketing, management techniques helped me spread the word about the book.

Surprisingly, it started to work, and there were many unknown people from different parts of India bumping into my Facebook page to read my posts. I believed the posts were catchy and very real that it caught their attention and I continued doing the same until the sales picked up a little pace. Now there were messages in my inbox from random people appreciating my work. That brought back a little hope in me.

So, I left no stone unturned in promoting my first novel.

After fifteen days, I started getting response for my book. People, who purchased my book and read it, wrote reviews online. Whenever a customer would order my book online, I would courier the book to the customer. So, within a span of one month, I was able to sell five hundred copies. This was an acceptance of my work, and it filled me with confidence. I started to focus more on my second book.

One day, I received a communication from Amazon. They told me that my book was selling like hot cakes and was in huge demand. It mentioned that the book had potential to be a bestseller in the near future. They asked me to deposit the copies of my book in bulk. So, I got my book published in bulk from the same vendor and handed it over to Amazon.

With the passage of time, my first novel became a big hit and it became a bestseller in India.

October 2015

I was sitting at the dining table with my parents and Garima. All of us were happy and I had tears in my eyes. But, this time these tears were of accomplishment, happiness and satisfaction. I had received a royalty cheque of fifteen lakh rupees for my first book. Neither I, nor my parents had expected such a great success with my first book. It was really a special achievement on my part after facing so many failures. So, when my first book became a bestseller, the publishers came back to me. At that time, I doubted their ability or intelligence of identifying the potential of a book.

My dreams came true for me after a long time due to my hard work and persistence in odd conditions. I had this god-gifted quality of writing since my childhood and now, for the first time in my life, I had realized my potential. So, I started to explore it to achieve my goals.

27

My dreams found wings

November 2016

Dreams are strange, amazing part of our life. I was merely twelve years old when I dreamt of being an author. My dreams had found wings now, and were ready to fly high. I had started tasting success. My novels were being published by famous publishers. My first novel created new sales records.

By November 2016, I had settled well enough to handle my own things; like finances, daily schedule and in fact, could afford a lot of things at that point of time. I mean why not! I had no girlfriends and no commitments to worry about. I was just dating myself; running at my own pace and enjoying life with my family in Gorakhpur.

So, after my first bestseller book, there was no looking back. I poured as much passion as possible in my work and the results were for everyone to see. My novels were gaining recognition and appreciation, rather quickly. I had written three novels so far. All three of them had been bestsellers and set new benchmarks of success in terms of sales and popularity. In a very short period of time, I reached at the peak of my thriving career which had remarkable future prospects. Of course, it was not so easy. In life, nothing commendable is easy to achieve. There were difficulties.

There were hurdles. Success tastes sweeter after struggle and pain. Dreams come true if you are dedicated to them.

Now, everything was changing. I loved my writing and it was 'love' that my writing dealt with. I wrote inspirational and motivational romantic novels. After all, everyone falls in love at least once in life. My readers were young and urbane. My romantic work would touch their hearts and lives.

It is a very important phase for an author when his career is picking up. All he thinks about is his work. Success and fame become his only targets. Everything else becomes secondary.

I was no exception and I focused all my attention on work. My work soared higher and success caressed me.

However, when I look back, I can never forget Aditi – everything about her was magical. I can still feel her with me, in my every breath.

I still can't understand how anyone can forget true love. I was trying hard to forget her. But couldn't.

I could still remember every small detail of the times we spent together. I never knew our love was so strong. She was and would always be my first love. There was still a part of my heart that wondered whether she really chose to go away from me. I had realized time can't be brought back. I needed to move on with my life.

Although we never met after that, I saw her face in various magazines every now and then as an upcoming young talent in singing. By now, she would have established herself as a reputed singer. I needed to forget all those moments of my life. I had to realize that Aditi was not coming back to me. She would be happy with her life.

I said to myself, *Someday you will forget about me, my name, and my voice, who I am and who I was to you. But still, I just want you to know that I will never forget a single thing about you and everything we went through. I can't jump into a new relationship just to try to erase you from my mind. I'm still ready to walk a million miles for you.*

One thing that I would always think of was: why did I let her go?

28

When life took a pleasant turn

March 2017

Now, almost two years had passed since I dropped out from DTU. I had become a bestselling author and it was quite satisfying for me. I had become well-known and a respected name among publishers. I also had started to write articles in various magazines and newspapers on issues related to youth of India, which became popular too.

Four months back, we had shifted to Udaipur due to my dad's posting. My younger sister Garima had got married a few months back, and her in-laws were in Jodhpur.

Udaipur is famous because of its attractive forts, royal palaces, beautiful gardens, clean lakes, and other monuments. Udaipur is also known as the 'City of Lakes'. It was the historic capital of the kingdom of Mewar.

I had a very busy schedule, thanks to my books. I had a spacious office in the front portion of my big house. I had hired a manager named Arvind and a team of two more persons – Kavita and Abhi – to look after various issues like finances, book editing, social media presence and fixing of meetings, etc. Either I used to write books or was busy with the publishers in book promotional events. These events used to be organized in various cities. So, I had to travel too. During such promotional events, I used to stay in hotels. I also gained a reputation as a young motivational speaker in several colleges and institutions. I used to address the issues related to youths and got a great response from my listeners.

February 2017, my fourth book was published and released in the market. I wrote a mythological fiction with the name *'Kalki'* based upon the perspective future tenth incarnation of my Lord Narayana. For this book, my publishers had arranged a number of promotional activities in all the leading cities of India. This was the same publisher who had outrightly rejected my first book. Readers had already pre-ordered my book through various online book stores. The book became popular within a week of its release. I received all round praise yet again for my fourth book

Amidst the success of book, in April 2017, I got an invitation to attend Jaipur Literature Festival. It was a great honour for a new and young author like me. I went to Jaipur with my manager Arvind to attend the festival and also to participate in my publisher's book promotional event for my latest book.

"Sir, let's move now. Our meeting with the publisher is in Malviya Nagar around 10:30 a.m. After that you have to attend the Literature Festival," Arvind reminded me.

I got up to leave; Arvind collected his handbag and called the driver.

Meanwhile, I was looking around, wondering if I should have eaten some tastier food. That was when I spotted a tall girl, her back towards me, at the other end of the coffee shop. If she wasn't tall, I wouldn't have noticed her. There were some other people with her. It seemed that she was about to leave. She turned towards the exit with her team. The waiter followed her to get a bill signed. She stopped and turned towards the waiter and I could see her face only for a few seconds. Yes, it was her: Aditi … Aditi Kohli.

Before I could have reacted, Aditi had left the restaurant.

"Sir, is she someone famous?" asked Arvind.

"No, nothing special," I said.

I asked Arvind to go and attend the meeting alone, and I would join later.

"Okay sir," said Arvind.

I walked towards the exit. I came to the lobby area, but she was not there. Was I wrong? I asked myself. No, I had seen her. The walk, the face, the height – there was only one Aditi. I rushed to the foyer in seconds and saw her leaving. The car windows were rolled up.

"Can I help you, sir?" a young hotel staff member at the concierge desk asked me.

"A girl has left just now. You saw her?" I asked him.

"Yes sir," the staff member replied.

"Where did she go? Has the hotel arranged a taxi for her?" I asked him.

"We don't know, sir. It's a private taxi."

"Will she be back?"

"Not sure, sir. Sorry. Is there a problem, sir?"

I shook my head. I walked back into the hotel, wondering what to do next. I went to the coffee shop again and found the waiter who was serving Aditi.

"You just gave a bill to that tall girl?"

"Yes, sir."

"She might be an old friend of mine. I'm trying to recognize her. Can I see that?"

The waiter went to the cash counter. He brought back the bill. I saw her signature. Yes, it was Aditi.

"Sir, she is staying in room no. 436, and her team in an adjacent three-star hotel," the waiter said.

I heaved a sigh of relief. I came to the reception and enquired about her.

"Yes, it is a booking in the name of a musical company. She is here for a week."

"When will she come back?"

"Can't say, sir. If you leave your name and number, we can ask her to contact you."

I wasn't sure if Aditi would do that. If I had to meet her, I had no choice but to wait. I decided to skip my meeting.

I sat in the hotel lobby, my eyes remained fixed on the entrance. I waited for almost ten hours. My eyes scanned every car arriving at the hotel.

At seven in the evening, Arvind returned. He looked exhausted.

After some formal talk, he left me in the lobby and went up to his room.

I pondered about what I would do if I happened to meet Aditi this night. But even then, I wanted to meet her so badly.

Around 8.00 p.m., I saw Aditi walking towards the entrance after bidding goodnight to her team. My heart started pounding; my mind started hovering, anxious to face Aditi. My eyes were fixed upon her .

A voice inside me advised me to run away; another voice convinced me to act.

Aditi didn't notice me. She directly went up to the reception.

Nervous, I wiped the sweat off my forehead with my hand. I cleared my throat and took a deep breath.

"436, please," she asked the receptionist.

The receptionist turned towards the key rack. Somehow, I put myself together and said to myself, *this is the right time and there is no point waiting.*

I walked to the reception quickly.

"Excuse me, which way is the coffee shop?" I asked, pretending.

"Oh my god," Aditi said. "Keshav!"

"Aditi… Aditi Kohli, am I right?" I said.

"Strange!! You have difficulty recollecting my name, Keshav!" Aditi said, with her eyes wide open.

"Aditi!" I said in a surprised tone.

The receptionist seemed surprised and amused at the happy coincidence right at her counter.

Aditi took her keys and we both stepped away from the counter.

"Great coincidence! What are you doing here in Jaipur, Keshav?" she said, walking with me.

"I have come here to participate in the Jaipur Literature Festival, and you?" I said.

"Okay, I have come here with my music team for an event," she said.

"What kind of event? Is it in Jaipur? You moved to Mumbai, right?" I asked so many questions one after another.

Aditi smiled and looked around the hotel lobby.

"Let's talk properly," she said.

"Okay."

"Have you had dinner?" she asked.

"No, I haven't," I replied.

"Let's go to the dining hall first," she suggested.

We sat at a corner table in the dining hall. Aditi ordered the food, as she knew my choice.

So, we had our first meal together in the last two years. The food had a special taste for me that night. The effect some people's mere presence can have on you is indescribable. Everything in the evening buffet tasted divine to me.

I kept silent for most of the time, worried I would say something stupid to upset her.

"You've become so quiet, suddenly," she said.

"Nothing like that," I said.

I looked at her. She was looking even more stunning than she had been in college days.

"So, I am meeting with the bestselling author of India, Mr Keshav Dixit, right?" she exclaimed.

"You know about that!!" I said, pleasantly surprised.

"Yes, although I am usually quite busy, I have read all your novels. I am a great fan of your writing skills," she said, with a smile on her face.

"Thanks Aditi, for admiring me. But I didn't expect you to have read my novels."

"In addition, I have read all your articles in newspapers and magazines too. I feel proud of you for all that," she said.

"Nice to know," I said.

"Now, tell me, what have you been up to?" I asked her.

Over the next fifteen minutes, she told me about her journey after leaving college. I kept on hearing, curiously.

"Tell me in detail," I said, intending to know about her personal life.

"I'll tell you everything in detail some other time, but I am not as popular as you," she said.

I smiled at her.

"It's not like that. I have seen your albums," I said.

She smiled.

Our eyes met. I tried to read her, considering she had said so little about herself. I did realize a touch of maturity in Aditi. I wanted to ask her about her personal life during the past few years. However, I couldn't ask her.

She also became quiet.

I wanted to touch her hand, but I restrained myself.

"How long are you in Jaipur for?" I asked.

"For a week," she said.

"Do you remember anything else, Aditi?"

"Anything, what?"

"About us?"

"Keshav…" she looked at me.

"Yes, our life in college?" I said.

"I've changed, Keshav," she took a deep breath and said. "In college, I was an immature, over-protected, idiotic eighteen-year-old girl with no clue about life, and overactive for achieving my dreams. We were all quite young back then."

I looked at her. I took a breath as if to control my feelings. She understood my pain and took my hand in hers. I felt secure. I felt like I was talking to a different Aditi altogether.

I kept quiet though.

"I am sorry Keshav. I know I had hurt you then. I was mad at that time to go to Mumbai, so all that happened. I didn't care for my parents' advice also. The last two years have taught me a lot," her unexpected apology startled me.

"What actually happened after my departure from DTU?" she asked, innocently.

"Let me avoid that for now," I said taking my eyes away from Aditi.

"What….?" she said.

"Nothing."

"Please tell me, Keshav, don't keep it in your heart."

"After you left DTU my life turned completely. I was out of track of everything; my study, my career, my placement and my dreams," I said in one breath.

"Oh, so sad. I over reacted then. And I've already apologized for everything in the past," she said with sad face.

I remained silent looking towards the entrance of the dining hall.

"Keshav, look at me," she said softly.

I turned my gaze back to her.

She smiled. I maintained a stern expression. She again took my hand in hers. I again felt as if our old days were back.

"But, how did you recover then?" she asked, with smile on her face.

Then I told her the complete story of my struggle, suicide attempt, rebuilding and recreating my life. I also told her about my current life, that my sister was married now and we lived in Udaipur.

She became serious and couldn't speak for a few minutes. I saw small drops of tears in the corner of her eyes. However, she masterfully hid her tears.

"So sad to know you couldn't complete your B.Tech. But, I am extremely happy to see you achieving your dreams, now. You are now the bestselling author that you dreamt of becoming ever since childhood," she said.

"Yes, but a still a long way to go in life," I said. "I am also glad to see you achieving your dreams. You are a popular singer now," I praised her.

"Thanks Keshav. I have come here to perform in a singing event along with my team."

I didn't say anything.

"Keshav, I am feeling so guilty now. In fact, I realized my mistake of losing you as a friend after joining music classes in Mumbai. I realized it is hard to find a true and trustworthy friend like you. I too missed our friendship in the last few years. I wanted to connect with you. I would think I was a phone call away from you, but, couldn't have the courage to talk to you. Would you like to be my friend again?" she said in a low and soft voice, looking straight into my eyes.

I remained silent. However, I could not refuse. "Yes, but on one condition," I said.

"What…?" she looked at my face.

"The condition is that you will always remain in touch with me, henceforth, like good friends. We can share life moments with each other, wherever we are," I said.

"Great! I would like us to be best friends and let's cooperate with each other. This time, I will not behave like an immature girl, I promise," she said.

"Really?"

"Yes, and I mean it."

"Did you get someone special? I mean a new friend in Mumbai?" I tried to clear my doubt.

"I have so many friends in Mumbai. But, no one could match you; your innocent friendship. You were special to me."

"Is it?"

"Yes, I'm saying it from my heart."

"It's okay then."

"Both of us are staying in the same hotel for a few days, so we can meet up after finishing our day's work. Maybe you can show me the city as I have come for the first time to Jaipur," she said.

"Sure, I'll do."

29

To me, you're still perfect

Suddenly destiny had taken another turn in my life and I had met Aditi.

I was elated. My life, sometimes, seemed so good, and sometimes so miserable.

We both finished our scheduled assignments in the next two days.

In the evening, she came back, exhausted.

"So, how was your event?" I asked.

"It was amazing; the Jaipur crowd is magnificent. It was a pleasant experience. And how was your speech at the festival?" she asked.

"That went well," I said.

"What about your fourth book? Is it doing well?"

"Yes, it is also going to be a bestseller as more than one lakh copies of the book have already been sold."

"One lakh copies within such a short time of its release! Wow, that's great!" she exclaimed.

The waiter arrived to take our order.

"I miss home food," she said.

I missed you, I wanted to say, but didn't. I wondered if we would ever get there as a couple. *Don't fall in love with her again*, a voice within me warned. *You never fell out of love with her*, another voice convinced me.

"Now, what's the plan?" she asked.

"You tell me; what do you want?" I said.

"I am quite tired after my event. So, I want to go to some beautiful place in Jaipur. Beautiful and peaceful maybe?" she said.

"Birla Mandir?" I said.

"Birla Mandir? I did not know there is one in Jaipur also?" Aditi said.

"Yes, there is," I told her about the famous temple.

"Okay, any other place?" she asked.

"There are so many places in Jaipur, like Hawa Mahal, City Palace, Amber Fort, Jantar Mantar Observatory, Jal Mahal, Chokhi Dhani and many more," I said.

"I want to visit a place which is very close to nature," she said.

"Okay, then let's go to Jal Mahal," I suggested.

"Jal Mahal?"

"Yes, Jal Mahal. If you are visiting this palace, you sure would enjoy the boat ride around the lake," I explained.

"Okay, then first we go to seek blessings of Lord Narayana in the Birla Mandir and then Jal Mahal," she finalized.

"Sure," I said.

So, from the hotel, we went ahead to seek blessings of Lord Vishnu in the Birla temple. It was surely a special moment for me to go to Birla Mandir with Aditi, after such a long time. We spent quite some time inside the temple. We were also lucky as we got to attend the aarti.

As we came out of the temple, I felt inner peace and satisfaction.

"Let's go to Jal mahal now," Aditi said.

"First, let's eat something," I proposed.

"What?

"Here, there is a superb place for pav bhaji which is very famous for tourists," I said.

"Okay," Aditi agreed.

After gratifying our appetite, we went to Jal Mahal.

The palace is partially submerged in the Man Sagar Lake. At night, the twinkling lights from inside the palace reflect beautifully on the lake.

We went for a boat ride in the lake. She held my hand to keep her balance as we tiptoed on the wooden plank towards the boat. She slipped a little and clasped my hand tighter. The sun had started to set. It turned the sky, the lake and Aditi's face into the colour of fire.

"It's so beautiful," Aditi breathed.

"Yeah, this is the most peaceful place in the city," I said.

The world seemed so beautiful to me, with Aditi by my side.

A cool evening breeze was blowing. It was an awesome experience watching the ripples of water, my hand inches away from hers. I wondered if she would be okay if I held it. But I restrained myself from doing that.

"So, you've started working on your fifth book?"Aditi asked.

"Sort of," I said.

"How was Mumbai?" I asked.

"Mumbai was quite nice. But I always like to live in Delhi. For me, Delhi, my hometown is the best place. I always miss Delhi wherever I live," she said.

"Should we go back?" I asked.

She nodded. We had reached the pier. The plank to the boat felt even more precarious in the darkness. She held my arm again. She seemed a little more vulnerable. Halfway through our journey, the temple bells began to ring in the distance. She placed her fingers on top of mine. I didn't turn towards her. I knew her. If I made an eye contact now, she would withdraw.

"I am more content and happy here, than Mumbai or Delhi," she said.

We reached the bank of the lake. I clasped her hand and held it until we got off the plank on to firm ground.

"Thank you so much. And I loved the boat-ride today."

"It's my pleasure."

"I am completely exhausted now," Aditi said.

We went to the room to have a little chit-chat.

"So, you have struggled a lot to become a famous author?" Aditi asked me.

"Yes, success comes like that. At one point, nothing seemed to work for me. But, I persisted and after some time, my hard work started to pay off," I said.

"I also struggled a lot in Mumbai to get recognition for my work," she said.

"Then how did you get a break in the music industry?" I asked.

"It's a long story, my struggle has been similar to you," she said.

"Okay, tell me that story about your struggle in Mumbai, how did you get yourself established over there?" I asked.

"Okay. I went to Mumbai and joined the music academy to further enhance my singing skills as a professional singer," she started and described her struggles in establishing herself as a singer.

30

Her struggles in her words

"I struggled a lot before I hit the spotlight. It was not so easy at all.

Living the rock-star life seems easy-peasy, but little do we realize that a lot of blood, sweat, tears and hard work have gone into getting that coveted spotlight.

When I left Delhi, I had already sung and performed in some schools and colleges in Delhi. I joined a prestigious music academy named *Geetmala* in Mumbai, for six months. There I learnt all the basics and essentials to sing a song professionally and become a professional singer. Life went smooth during the six months of my training in *Geetmala*. During the training, I would think that I would get a break immediately as a singer just after completing my singing classes.

But, that never happened.

After completing the training, I strolled around and tried hard to get a break as I was confident of my voice and my talent. But, I couldn't get a break. After some time, I got a chance to sing for a musical group. They needed a singer badly. I appeared in their trial. The manager of the group was not happy with my trial performance. He fired me and advised me to go back to college and study since he felt that I was not talented enough for the music industry.

I was disappointed. I talked to my parents and cried.

My parents and brother visited me in Mumbai and consoled me and stayed with me for a few days. My mom was very worried to see me struggling so much in Mumbai. My parents, especially my father, were backing me financially and emotionally in a strong way to make sure I fulfill my dreams.

So, in a span of one year, I learned music and singing from fifteen different music teachers. Most of my teachers felt that I was hopeless and wouldn't have a career in singing.

I have lived a life of disgrace there that I could never have imagined.

I would stand outside music directors' offices for hours without any food or water. I faced a lot of humiliation and had a lot of insecurities before getting my actual breakthrough.

Those lessons made me more determined, and so, I persisted despite all odds against me. My passion for music continued unhindered. Then I started to sing independently. I advertise myself as a solo singer.

To the good fortune of my hard work and struggle, my passion won. The effortless modulation of my voice and its immense range took me places. I got a chance as a playback singer for a Marathi film. The movie was successful.

After that I sang in almost ten Marathi films and theatres in various studios in Mumbai.

However, soon I realized that I needed to do something different to go higher in my career.

After discussing with my parents, I decided to start my own rock-star band. My father was ready to bear all heavy expenses to start a band in Mumbai.

The first step to starting a successful band was to find the musicians – a guitarist, a drummer, a music composer, and a bassist are required. There should also be a lead singer who may or may not need to play an instrument.

During my struggle as a playback singer in Marathi films, I came in touch with so many struggling artists in the music industry. So, I met them and made a group to launch a rock-star band. I was the only female in the band and a lead singer. I was the founder and organizer of the band as I bore all the expenses; courtesy to my father who stood firm behind her daughter in every situation. We chose the name *Indian Rockstars* for the band. We took a big place on rent to practice. In the front part, we made an office to serve marketing purposes.

It is said that practice makes a man perfect and this was perfectly applicable for a band which needed to rehearse together as much as possible to develop a good rapport that would be their hallmark in their future and help them become successful. Proper practice also comes in handy when bands go to record their songs.

After a lot of practice, we recorded a demo of our band. Now, we were looking for shows. So, we advertised with the help of pamphlets and newspapers. We also posted our demo on various music websites, social networking sites like Facebook and YouTube.

But, even after good efforts of my team, our band didn't get a chance to showcase our talent. Nobody hired us to perform in their events.

We didn't lose hope even in such a disappointing situation.

We then decided to offer shows to audience, free of cost.

We also asked our friends, relatives and acquaintances to get some word of mouth publicity.

Soon, our hard work began to pay off. We started to receive invitations from schools and colleges to organize free shows at their venues.

Initially, we were happy to offer free shows as at least we got a chance to showcase our talent in front of an audience. I got special attraction of youth wherever we went to perform, as I was the lead singer.

I would love to perform and connect with people.

My band had done almost twenty shows for free. I gained confidence to organize live shows.

Later on, I used social media to turn my followers into friends. Twitter, Facebook, Instagram – they not only actually got me new fans, but they allowed me to interact with them also.

Initially, I answered each person's tweet, comment and message. These people believe in you and most likely care about what you care about, which is so precious and beautiful. Everyone has a gift to share and you will likely learn and hear amazing art and ideas from them too.

The listeners from social media became my base and would want to interact with me. So, I was always ready for them and replied to them. This way, I built a music community.

It was an amazing practice. After that I reached a point where I felt enormous confidence in organizing live shows in front of a large audience.

So, after organizing free shows, our band became quite famous and we started to get paid shows.

An important milestone was 2017 release of *Take a Breath* album of our band on which my unusual song of the same name won me praise as a solo singer.

Although I first gained fame as a playback singer in Marathi films, then with the help of live shows of my band and then release of my famous album, I was soon roped in to sing for films and jingles in Hindi as well as various regional languages.

Today, I sing in Hindi films as well.

I am grateful to my parents and my brother Gaurav for supporting me in such a hard time.

Aditi took a deep breath.

I had a lot of praise in my eyes for her, after knowing her struggle to achieve her dreams.

"Keshav, these kinds of struggles teach us a lot of lessons in life. I too learnt some special things during my hard days in Mumbai."

"Like?"

"Like, all those bad experiences had made me very humble and soft. Earlier, I would overreact to a silly matter, but, now I don't lose temper so easily and consider every aspect of any situation. Further, it also made me learn to respect people who are close to you and care for you, especially your parents, other family members and true friends. I realized it is very difficult to find a true friend. Keshav, that was the time I really missed you. I would think I had lost a gem in Keshav due to my over possessive and over-reactive attitude. So, now I can admit my greatest wealth is my family and a true friend like you!" Aditi said and took a deep breath.

Hearing all this, I felt honored and emotional for Aditi. I couldn't speak for a few minutes.

Some people say that love is the most underrated concept. Some say it is overrated. I would say that it is just the language that every heart understands, and craves for throughout their lives. It is the feeling one gets after finding an oasis after days of walking in the scorching heat of a desert. It is the concept that can win dynasties, which can make a beggar the richest person in this entire universe. When you are in love, this world stands still. And at that moment, mine was perfectly still in Aditi's room.

She looked breathtakingly beautiful that night. In fact, she seemed beautiful, more than ever. All that I ever wanted to do was to kiss her hard. I wanted to scream at her telling how much I love her; how important she was to me. Nobody in the entire universe mattered to me more than her. She was divine. Yes, I wanted to make love to her. Oh! How beautiful she looked! But, I was helpless. Helpless in a way nobody would ever understand. Helpless in a way even I couldn't help myself. I wanted to take her with me and elope forever in a world where nobody could find us; in a world, where it'd be just me and her. But would she ever accept me as her life partner?

Aditi was smart enough to observe my feelings.

To make me feel better, she changed the topic, "So, you are taking me to your home in Udaipur?"

"Yes, I want that."

"But, why?"

"Because, there is a function at my place, this Sunday."

"Okay, today is Thursday, but, what's the occasion?"

"Occasion is the enormous nationwide success of my fourth book. My parents want to celebrate these moments. They want to share their happiness with relatives and friends."

"Will it be okay for me to go there?"

"Yes, why not? I'll proudly introduce you and your success story with my parents."

"Okay, I'll come then."

"Thanks, so let's be ready early in the morning tomorrow."

"Sure."

I said goodnight to Aditi and came out of her room.

We had to go to Udaipur the next morning.

31

She visited my place in Udaipur

Next day, we had our breakfast early in the morning and took a direct flight from Jaipur to Udaipur.

"Keshav, are you sure your parents will be okay with me staying over at your house for a day or two?"she asked.

"Of course," I said.

We were riding in a cab from Udaipur airport to my home. She wore a fitted white T-shirt and black tights. Although fully covered, the snug outfit highlighted her curves.

During cab ride, I asked her, "Will you sing a song for me now?"

"You want me to?" she asked.

"Do you want to?" I asked back.

She nodded and smiled at me. As she hummed one line of my favourite song '*Zindagi kaisi hai paheli*...' I was lost in old memories of my college days when Aditi used to sing lots of songs for me. Those college days were the most beautiful days of my life. I would not trade them for anything in the world.

Soon, we reached home.

I didn't find my parents at home. I rang Mom. She told me that they had come for a get together of some old family friend in the outskirts of Udaipur and would return in the evening.

I couldn't believe Aditi was in my home in Udaipur. I wanted to kiss her. I thought how mind-blowing that would be.

"What are you thinking now?" She snapped her fingers.

Her question made me freeze.

"Huh? Nothing! Lunch? Should we have lunch?" I asked.

"Oh, yes."

We ate the lunch together and after that I showed my home to Aditi. I also introduced Aditi to my staff in the office.

"Wow, it's quite peaceful here."

"Udaipur itself is a peaceful place," I said.

"Is she here?" my mother asked.

"Yes," I said.

I met my parents in the courtyard of the house as they came back.

"Where is she?" asked my dad.

"In the guest room."

"Girls are very strange these days. Go, live in whichever boy's house," Mom said looking at dad's face.

"What are you saying, mom? She is a friend from college. I invited her over here," I said.

"But, she is the same girl who destroyed your college life," mom said, with a stern expression on her face.

"Mom, she has become mature enough now."

"Do her parents know?" my dad asked.

"I don't know."

My mother shook her head.

"Be nice to her, Mom," I requested.

"You still like her?" Mom asked.

"What kind of a question is that, mom?" I said.

"Keshav, we can't forget the wounds she has given to you and of course to us as well," mom said, sounding betrayed.

"I need to take a bath," I said, changing the topic.

It took me fifteen minutes to bathe. I came down to the living room.

Aditi and my parents were already there.

"You met already?" I said looking at Aditi.

"Hi, I was just chatting with uncle and aunty," Aditi said.

"You had a tour in Jaipur with her?" my mother asked me.

"Well, she was in Jaipur too with her team for an event. So, we met in the hotel," I said.

"You never mentioned her. You used to talk so much with us while in Jaipur," my mother questioned me.

"I didn't?" I said, pretending to be surprised.

"No," my mother said, looking straight at my face.

"We were only together for three days," I said, trying to justify.

Aditi and I looked at each other.

My mother turned to Aditi.

"So, beta, are you married or not?" Mom asked Aditi.

My mouth fell open. *What the hell? What is mom talking about?*

"Not yet," she said.

"Why?" Mom asked again.

Aditi told her story, in short.

"Why did you leave your education and home so early? What motivated you to go to Mumbai?" my mother asked.

Mom obviously had no filter in her head on what to ask or not.

"I was mad about becoming a singing star. I used to think only about music in my college days. Engineering was not my first choice; I got admission in engineering according to the will of my family," Aditi said.

"Where are your parents?"

"Delhi."

"They let you go to Mumbai and all other places for your live shows? They have a big business in Delhi? Okay, you are from a rich family. Why are you working?" Mom asked her so many questions one after another.

"They don't let me do things. I wanted to. I can decide for myself. Their first choice for me was to stay back at home and after engineering, be a part of the family business. But, I was adamant about pursuing my dreams. I wanted to be independent. So, my father had no choice but to support me," Aditi said.

"Okay, very nice to know about your dream," mom said.

"Beta, how did you get success as a singer in Mumbai? As far as I know, it's quite difficult to make your own identity in Mumbai for a newcomer," my father asked.

"Uncle, you are right. I struggled a lot. But, I was confident and persisted," Aditi said looking at me. I felt proud.

"So, both of you have similar stories. I think it's a lesson for parents like us. In fact, for all parents, to identify the passion of their kids and let them flourish in the area of their interests. Parents should not force their will on kids, rather support them to achieve their dreams," Papa said.

"Yes, uncle, after some time, the passion becomes the livelihood," Aditi said.

"We are proud of you beta, your ideas are great. I think only one out of a thousand girls can think like you. You will go a long way in your life," Papa praised her.

"Uncle, Keshav has also achieved remarkable success in becoming a leading author of India," Aditi said.

"Yes, we are also proud of him, but, that has come after lot of bad times, grief and family disturbance," my mother said.

Aditi had no answer. She took her eyes away from Mom.

I decided to change the topic.

"Aditi wanted to see Udaipur, particularly Jagdish Temple. In fact, I called her home for that," I interfered deliberately.

"Oh, really?" Mom asked, surprised.

"Yes, Aunty, Keshav has taken me several times to Lord Narayana Temple in Delhi in college days," Aditi said in excitement.

"Oh?" my mother said looking at me, one eyebrow raised.

"Well, a few times," I said, my tone guilt-ridden again. "Twice or thrice. We went only when we got time from studies."

"We thought you went there to study," Mom said.

I didn't reply. I wished I had told her more about Aditi, but I could never gather the courage.

"Okay beta, we have a small family function on Sunday to celebrate the success of Keshav. You also attend that function and stay here for a few more days," Papa said.

"It's my pleasure uncle."

"Should I arrange dinner on the dining table?" I said.

"I can also do that," Aditi said.

My mother looked at her.

"If it's okay? I know the kitchen. I can help Usha aunty," Aditi said. Usha aunty used to cook for us.

My mother shook her head. Aditi took it as assent and left.

"Now I understand why you used to be so reluctant to come home in semester breaks," Mom said once Aditi was out of earshot.

"It's not what you think, Mom. Now, I consider Aditi just as a friend, an old classmate. We have decided to be in touch in future like good friends," I said, hiding my feelings for Aditi.

"Now, she seems to be a good girl to me. I think her struggle in Mumbai has taught her a lot. Be nice to her," my mother advised.

"I am nice. She is staying in my house. What else do you want me to do?" I rolled my eyes.

"Why is she wearing such tight clothes?" she said next.

"I have no idea, mom," I said, my voice loud. "I don't know why she wears tight clothes. Can you let her be?"

Papa remained silent.

"You are shouting at your mother for her?" My mother looked away from me. It was mom's classic sulky face.

"I'm not shouting," I said, my voice still too loud to classify it as anything else.

My mother looked away.

I realized I needed her cooperation to have a peaceful dinner.

"Sorry," I said. Mom sniffed.

En route to the dining room, with a stack of plates, Aditi smiled at me. I smiled back.

"I said sorry, Mom," I said after Aditi went back to the kitchen.

My mother glared at me, "Keshav, you know we've already suffered enough in life. Don't add to it."

"I won't," I said.

"Your mom is right, Keshav beta. We can't forget those painful days. That was the most difficult time for all of us in the family. We were rushing to doctors here and there for your treatment," Papa added.

"And all that happened due to this girl only," Mom said.

"Mom, that was a different time. Now, both of us are not so emotional, rather matured enough. We are moving ahead in our golden career," I said, trying to convince my parents.

"We are proud of you beta. We are not against any of your decisions. We also like Aditi. We have understood that she is ambitious in life and wants to become a star on her own, just like you, that's why there is still a good mutual and emotional bonding between you and her. We are only advising you to take decisions in your future life, wisely, and not from the heart," Dad said.

"And, we are not against her as well. We like her and respect her efforts in life. Rather, we are feeling some unknown happiness and positive energy since she has come here." Mom smiled for the first time.

"Okay, I'll follow your advice from my heart and soul," I convinced both of them.

"Dinner's served," Aditi said, clapping her hands in the dining room.

We had a peaceful dinner. I felt relaxed as soon as the two ladies became comfortable with each other. They bonded well. All my mother wanted was a girl who was well-mannered, belonged to a good family, and above all, who could keep me happy.

My father too gelled with Aditi instantly, as he did with all my other friends.

"Aditi, don't feel bad and worry about my mother," I said.

"I'm not. Why should I be worried?" she said and smiled at me. "All mothers are the same, I guess."

"She's not bad at heart," I said.

"I know. Did she mention something about me when I went to the kitchen?"

"Not really. Why?"

"My clothes, my lifestyle, anything?"

"Nothing important," I said.

My study room was well furnished with all the modern day necessities and latest electronic gadgets. However, the walls still were lined with certificates and pictures.

"So many certificates?" she said as she scanned them.

"There are two types of certificates; one for academic excellence and other for winning essay and other writing competitions. They began right from the primary school, those I had won in class VI to the one I had won in 12th standard," I told her.

"How about family pictures?" she said.

I opened my study table drawer. I took out a photograph of the DAV School's annual day. My mother stood on a stage along with me.

"Your mom?" she said, holding the picture.

"Yes," I smiled.

"You have more pictures?"

"Not really," I said and rifled through the drawers. I found another black-and-white photo, but hid it.

"What is that?"

"Nothing."

"Show me that picture."

"No, it's a childhood picture."

"Oh, then I definitely want to see it." She charged towards me.

"No," I protested and tried to shut the drawer.

She laughed, and tickled me like she did in college. I wanted to grab her tight, but didn't do that. I surrendered, let her have the picture and stepped aside. She looked at it and began to laugh like anything.

"How old are you in this?"

"Four years old."

Aditi sat down on the bed. She examined the photograph like a detective solving a murder mystery. I sat next to her.

"Is that your old house in Gorakhpur?" she said.

I nodded.

"It's beautiful."

"That's nineteen years ago."

"It's a cool place. I wish I could see Gorakhpur, I'd love to go and see it."

I laughed.

"What?" she said, puzzled.

"You? In Gorakhpur?"

"Yeah, why not?"

I shook my head and laughed again.

"What's so funny about it?" she said and tickled me.

"Aditi, stop it. I'm ticklish," I said and laughed uncontrollably.

"You think I can't leave my sheltered life?" she said, poking my stomach with her fingers.

I grabbed and held her. She realized it only after a few seconds.

"Hey," she said.

"What?"

"You're holding me."

"Good observation." I looked straight into her eyes.

She did not look away. She released herself from my grip and shifted to the study chair.

"Come here. Near me," I said.

"No, sir. I don't trust you."

"Really? Your best friend?"

"Who is not behaving like a friend," she said, emphasizing the last word.

I lay back on the bed, dangling my legs.

She rolled her eyes, stood up and came to sit down next to me.

"No girl has ever meant more to me than you."

She laughed.

"What?"

"That could mean two things. I am really special, or there's not been much choice."

I couldn't answer. I bent forward and gave her a light peck on her lips. Her lips felt soft and warm. I gave her another peck. She placed her hand on my chest and pushed me back.

"What?" I said.

"Your mother is downstairs," she said.

I took her words as encouragement. She did not say no; she only mentioned my mother.

"She's asleep," I said.

I entwined my fingers with hers. She didn't protest. I turned my face towards her. She freed her hand and slid a few inches away.

"Let's watch TV!" she said.

It's unique, the grace with which girls can deflect situations and topics.

"Not now, I'm tired," I said.

"Should we go downstairs then?" Aditi said, all innocence.

I looked into her eyes. She understood that look. We had shared it years ago in college. I leaned forward, my lips an inch from hers.

"No, Keshav, no," she said and gently placed her hand on my chest.

However, she didn't push me away, her fingers were directly over my heart, I leaned back a bit.

"Why not?" I said.

"We agreed to be just friends, no more."

"So what?"

"Don't ask me such questions. You know me, what I like, what I don't."

But, I didn't stop, I leaned over again. This time, she pushed me back.

"Don't do this. Please," her eyes were now wet.

I felt guilty. I withdrew immediately.

"Can we at least talk?" She urged.

"We are talking."

"Keshav, you are a nice guy. An amazing guy, okay?"

"If you say so," I said.

"But…"

"There's always a *but*."

"Can we please restrain ourselves from doing all this?"

"Okay, I'm not good enough for you?" I asked.

She smiled.

"What?" I said.

"I just said you are an amazing guy."

We stayed silent for a minute.

"I can't live without you, Aditi," I said.

She turned to me. She held my hand. I pulled it away.

"Stop sulking, my bestselling author," she said.

"One kiss," I said.

"What?"

"Just one kiss. After that I promise we will be friends. Just friends."

"How does that work for you?"

"I don't know. I can't get that one kiss out of my head. I need to know I mean something to you. I understand your situation. I won't expect anything. I will be a friend and value you as one. But just one kiss for now."

"But…"

"Please…" I said and kept my hand on her mouth.

I came forward. Her eyes blinked in surprise. I removed my fingers. My lips landed on hers. We kissed for the first time. She put her arms around me as if to keep her balance. The kiss was light at first, and then picked up intensity. She buried her face in my shoulder. More than kisses, I could tell she wanted to be held, as if she had not hugged anyone in a really long time. I held her tighter, landing kisses wherever I could, on her face, neck, lips.

After few minutes, she stirred.

"That lasted a while?" she said.

"What?"

She smiled at me.

"What….?" I looked into her eyes.

"It was nice," she said taking her gaze away from me.

"What was?"

"What we just did."

"That was nice?" I said.

"Yes," she said and laughed.

I wanted to touch her, but didn't. I couldn't believe I had kissed Aditi.

Some time later, she coughed. Once, twice…. and then five more times.

"Are you okay, Aditi?"

"Yeah, it is a little cold," she said and went into a coughing fit.

"I'll get water for you," I ran downstairs to kitchen.

I came back with a bottle of water. She lay on the sofa, right hand on her forehead.

"You're not well, Aditi?" I said, worried.

She coughed again, sat up and had some water. I touched her forehead.

"You don't have fever," I said,

"I'm exhausted, I guess," she said.

"Did I stress you out by kissing?" I said.

I felt extremely guilty about kissing her.

"No. I just need rest."

She had a coughing fit again, this time more violent. I helped her stand up and escorted her to the guest room.

"Will you be okay here? You want someone here? I could wake up mom," I said.

She smiled. "No, no, please. I need sleep, that's all. We are going to the Jagdish temple tomorrow morning, right?"

"If you're feeling better, only then," I said, worried.

"I'll be okay. Goodnight, Keshav," she said.

"Goodnight, Aditi," I said, not wanting to leave though.

"Thanks for taking care of me," she said, her voice sleepy.

She shut the door.

"I love you, Aditi," I whispered before I drifted off to sleep.

So, the next morning, we went together to Jagdish temple – one of the famous temples of Udaipur. We visited the entire temple. It was indeed peaceful inside. "I really love the holy atmosphere here," Aditi said.

"Yes, it's definitely a must visit place in Udaipur," I said.

"Have you come here earlier?"

"Yes, so many times, I don't remember. I have attended evening aarti, also."

"Oh, next time, if I come here, I'll definitely attend evening aarti."

She was still staying in my house and was rehearsing her music. I realized, she just couldn't stay without music.

After rehearsal, she sat next to me and held my hand. She coughed again. I was sad to see her in pain.

"What happened to you? Is Udaipur climate not suiting you," I said, worried.

"I don't know. It's an allergy. Something in the air. Can't figure out what's making it flare up. I think it might be a throat infection."

"So, don't rehearse further and take rest."

Aditi smiled. "Let's eat lunch," she said.

Post lunch, we came back to the living room. My parents also came there. We all were discussing some random stuff.

Meanwhile, Aditi's phone rang. She took the call. It was her father. She became serious while talking on phone.

"Keshav, I have to go to Delhi, urgently."

"Why? What happened?" Mom asked her, worried.

"Aunty, it was my dad. Mom is unwell. She wants to meet me. So, I have to go to Delhi to see my mom."

"Okay beta, then you go. We will reschedule our function according to your availability here in Udaipur," mom said.

"Aunty, no need to change the date. I'll go by flight to Delhi tonight. After staying for one day with my mom, I'll return on Sunday morning to attend the function."

"It will suit us," Papa said.

"Do you need anyone of us to go with you?" my father further asked.

"No, uncle, I'll manage."

"Keshav, arrange everything for Aditi, right now," Mom told me.

Aditi left Udaipur that night to go to Delhi to see her mother.

So, on Sunday, everything was well arranged for the function at my house in the evening.

Aditi too, had come back from Delhi to celebrate my success. I felt refreshed to see Aditi back.

I thanked god!

The function was organized in the big party hall in the outhouse. Our house was tastefully decorated with flowers, bunting and balloons. The house looked as if it was a place in paradise. The seating arrangement was made under a very big canopy. The best band of the city created sweet sensations by its tunes of modern films.

Aditi enjoyed the music the most.

My parents were greeting guests at the entrance of the house. Aditi and I were standing in the middle of the hall. All the guests were greeting me with congratulations. I introduced Aditi as my friend.

Suddenly, I heard some disturbance from the entrance side. My father came towards me.

"Keshav, some reporters from Delhi have come to take your interview," Dad said in pleasant tone.

"But, dad, I don't think it is a suitable time for an interview."

"You are right, but this is the first time that a national news channel has shown interest in your interview," he said.

I remained silent.

"Yes Keshav, uncle is right. This is a golden opportunity for you. These are the chances by which you can increase your fan following," Aditi said.

"Beta, the function is going on and everything will run smoothly. You please be ready for the interview. It will be good for your career ahead. You may keep Aditi with you while being interviewed," Papa emphasized.

"Okay, Papa."

So, within a few minutes, I sat down on sofa chairs in one corner of the hall along with Aditi. The reporters took twenty minutes to install their setup for the interview. Almost eight persons from various news channels sat in front of me.

According to me, it was not an interview; rather, it was a press conference cum interview. Anyway, I was glad to talk to the reporters with Aditi sitting beside me. While building up for interview, one female reporter recognized Aditi as an upcoming singer in Bollywood. After all, Aditi was also a star like me.

Reporter: Mr Keshav, first of all, we are happy that we also have Ms Aditi, a singing star, before us. How do you know each other?

Aditi: Actually, Keshav and I are old classmates and good friends, that' why I'm here.

Reporter: But, as far as we know, you live in Mumbai?

Aditi: Yes, in fact, I live in Delhi. But, due to my singing assignments, currently I'm living in Mumbai.

Reporter: So, you have travelled directly from Mumbai to Udaipur to be a part of this party?

Aditi: Actually, I had come to Jaipur to perform in a live show, along with my team. So, I have come here from Jaipur to celebrate his success.

Reporter: Okay, Ms Aditi. Thank you. Now, we would like to hear from you, Mr Keshav. How are you feeling after the great success of your fourth book?

Me: Yeah, I'm feeling great. It was like a dream come true. I am grateful to my readers.

Reporter: You have written your first three books on love and romance and those books were very successful. But, why have you chosen to write this one on mythological fiction? What motivated you to write a mythological fiction book instead of a book on youth this time?

Me: No, it's not like that. This book also has certain messages for Indian youth. Actually, I am a religious and spiritual person, so I got inspiration for writing this book from Lord Vishnu.

Reporter: Tell us something about your book *Kalki*?

Me: It's difficult to summarize an epic novel into a few sentences, but I will try. I took some inspiration from other major epic stories such as Mahabharata and created my own epic story. The mythological idea of *Kalki* has existed since thousands of years and has been described in *Kalki Purana*, but the subject was never been explored in details. This is what prompted me to make *Kalki* as the primary theme of my book.

Reporter: Did you face any problems with publishing your first book? How did you get a break in the industry?

Me: Yes, I have. Initially, I had faced many problems with publishers. Most publishers don't care to read your book until you are famous. Most publishers would just look at your background and deny publishing your book. I faced so many rejections from publishers even when there were also the ones that supported me. Since I was not satisfied with the response of publishers, I decided to launch my book on my own.

Reporter: What has been the response from readers and your family?

Me: My family has been supportive since the beginning and continues to do so. My father has always supported me and he always reads my books. However, he was not impressed with Kalki, since he is more of a Sidney Sheldon fan. But that is not a problem since my target audience is the youth and my book is meant for them only.

Reporter: Do you have any upcoming books?

Me: I have two books in the pipeline. These would again be devoted to Indian youth and their issues, and the new changing India. Both the books are expected to be published in 2020.

Reporter: Ms Aditi, tell us about your journey as a singer? Your first album has been quite famous.

Aditi: My struggle, more or less, has been the same as that of Keshav. You know it's not easy for a Delhi resident to go to Mumbai and become a star in one night. I have spent days of disappointment, hopelessness and hard work before getting a break to sing in a Marathi film.

Reporter: Okay, so, Mr Keshav and Ms Aditi, what is your future plan about your personal life? Will you take your friendship to the next level or what?

Aditi and I felt awkward at the sudden question about our personal life. There was a pin drop silence for a few seconds. Before I could say anything, Aditi responded.

Aditi: See, it's not like that. We have been classmates and are good friends now to help each other. Right now, both of us are focusing on our career. So, it's nothing like what you are thinking.

All the media persons smiled at Aditi's diplomatic answer and the interview was completed, after some more questions.

As soon as the interview got completed, the crowd roared in excitement. All the guests stood up and continued to clap. My mother gave me a hug. Dad came up to me and whispered in my ear, "Congratulations, Keshav, you did it well."

"It's all your blessings, Papa!"

"Thank you, Keshav Sir," a young guy from my neighbourhood tried to touch my feet.

"You are our hero, sir," said another.

I wanted to bring Aditi and my parents for some pictures on stage. But the crowd wouldn't let me get past them. The crowd lifted me in jubilation.

Aditi was looking at all this with a lot of amusement.

After the function and the interview, Aditi came to my study room.

"So, it was a great day for you today. You will appear on national TV now," Aditi said with a pleasant expression on her face.

"Oh, yes, indeed! It was a great time for me. But, you will also become a national star after this interview on TV."

"Yes, but it all happened due to the massive success of your fourth book."

"Yeah, I think, this interview will take us a long way in our respective careers."

"Definitely."

Aditi coughed again. I got her a glass of warm water.

"Aditi, tomorrow, I have a book promotion event in Udaipur itself. That's important for me and already planned a long time back. As soon as I come back after the event, your treatment is my first priority. We need to find a good doctor, either here in Udaipur or Delhi," I said, emphasizing on my words.

"I'm fine. See, it's okay now," she said and took some medicine with water.

She shut her eyes and patted the mattress, signalling for me to sit next to her. She then put her head on my lap, taking a deep breath, as if she was fighting the pain inside. I felt anxious to see her condition.

"You want to sleep here?" I asked.

She didn't say anything. I got a pillow and blanket. She smiled in gratitude, with eyes closed.

"Okay, I'm tired too. I'm going, will sleep downstairs," I spoke slowly.

She shook her head, gestured at me to not go and sit with her.

I wondered to myself. What did she want? Did she want me to stay with her?

"Should I stay here?" I asked, still standing.

She didn't say anything, still kept her eyes closed with pain on her face.

"Okay, I'll stay here for some more time," I said, worried seeing her condition.

She nodded in agreement.

She moved aside, eyes still shut, making space for me. I was shocked. Aditi actually wanted me to lie down with her. I slid in next to her, as quietly as possible, keeping a certain distance from her.

"Are you sleeping?" I asked her.

She nodded in agreement.

A caring relation doesn't require a long conversation. A soft message is enough, because it's not the mouth that speaks!! It's the heart that feels.

I shut my eyes. But, I could not sleep. I was much worried now to see her condition. What had happened to her health? Normal cough doesn't give so much pain. I cursed myself for not taking her to the doctor today, instead I remained busy in my function and interview. I should have taken her health seriously.

I wanted to hold her close. I wanted to kiss her hard. I placed an arm around her. I didn't have courage to do anything else. Maybe, this way she was getting comfortable with me, I said to myself. Aditi's smooth arm around me, made me feel uncomfortable.

So, I turned to my side. Meanwhile, she slept.

Intimacy is not purely physical; it's the act of connecting with someone so deeply, you feel like you can see into their soul.

Sleeping next to someone you love makes you fall asleep faster, reduces depression, and helps you live longer.

However, I couldn't sleep that night.

I kept on thinking so many things.

I muttered, *I'm glad that I met you, Aditi. You're the best part of my life. Please, now, stay forever. You are my everything, you're my happiness.*

Aditi was sleeping. Now, pain on her face seemed to have subsided. I felt relaxed on seeing that. I didn't move as I didn't want to disturb her.

It was 11 o' clock in the night, when Aditi opened her eyes, slowly.

"You are still awake, didn't sleep at all?" she said, sleepily.

"No, I couldn't sleep. I was thinking something."

"I understand."

"Okay, now, you take complete rest. I'm going downstairs to sleep," I said, rolling out of the bed.

As I got up, she again held my hand.

"What..."

"Keshav, I'm feeling afraid and alone tonight, maybe due to the medicine. I want someone to stay with me during the night. I'm badly missing my mom, tonight," she said in slow voice.

"Okay, let me send my mom to you."

"No, please... you stay here, I'm comfortable with you. Now, you sleep, I'll stay up. I'll enjoy music with my headphones."

I wondered what had happened to her, her health. She was feeling so vulnerable. Was she afraid of a coughing fit again?

"Okay, you please take rest and sleep. I'll sleep there on the sofa," I said.

"Will it be alright for you?"

"Yes, it's almost 11:30. I'll have to sleep for only five to six hours, I will manage.

"Okay, I'm disturbing you so much. I'm sorry, Keshav."

"Don't say that."

"Thanks, Keshav," she said and closed her eyes again.

However, I just couldn't sleep. I was thinking about her.

Why was she feeling afraid and vulnerable?

I had always seen Aditi as a strong girl. She had been my inspiration. I couldn't see her pleading that way.

32

I was left stranded again

So, next morning, I went to attend a book promotional event, although worried for Aditi' health.

I returned around 2 pm in the afternoon.

As soon as I entered, I saw a lot of people inside. Some of them were my distant relatives and some were neighbours and local friends of my parents. I guessed all of them had come to congratulate me and my parents, after watching my interview on TV. My parents were surrounded by so many people. Finding me there, everybody started to congratulate me.

Where was Aditi, I asked myself. Was she still resting in the guest room or in my study room?

I looked around frantically. There was no sign of her.

I went upstairs in my study room, I didn't find her. I peeped into the guest room but the room was empty. I searched her on the second and third floor and also on the terrace, but she was not there.

Where did she go? I wondered.

I came downstairs, into the hall. By now, the crowd had thinned. My mother came to me, "What happened, Keshav? Why are you so worried?"

"Mom, have you seen Aditi?" I said, nervous.

"No, I have not seen her for quite some time," Mom shook her head.

I couldn't find Aditi in the outhouse also.

I called Aditi on he mobile. Nobody picked up.

I tried again. Twice, thrice. No response!

I called up Aditi's driver in Jaipur.

"I am on leave, sir. Madam must have taken another driver," he said.

I hung up. I wondered what to do next.

Where could she have gone? Did she get an urgent call from home? Office? Mumbai? Where could she be?

"Keshav sir," a girl's voice interrupted my chain of thoughts. It was Kavita, my colleague from the editorial staff. "Keshav sir, Aditi ma'am had left something for you," Kavita handed me a white envelope. "She left around 9 a.m., while you were out."

"Did she tell you where she was going?"

Kavita shook her head.

"Did she go in a car?"

Kavita nodded. I tore open the envelope.

"Where are you?" my mother shouted from a distance.

"Here only," I said.

I slipped the envelope into my pocket.

"Many people have come home to celebrate. Come, let's have lunch."

"Mom, I need to go upstairs to my room."

"Why? What about your lunch?"

"I'm tired. I'll have it later."

I ran upstairs and shut the door. I took out the letter from the envelope.

Dear Keshav,

I want you to remain calm and composed when you read this. I am writing this letter to tell you something important.

My fingers are shaking as I write this. I must stay strong. I have to type my parting note, feeling so bad. I am feeling very low, however, I want to tell you how I feel about you…

Keshav, I am leaving Udaipur. I am not well. I think you noticed my cough over the past few days. It is not an infection or allergy. My vocal cord has been damaged due to excessive singing; that's what the doctors have diagnosed in Mumbai. This is a severe throat disease. Doctors have advised me, fifteen days back, to go for immediate surgery to fix my damaged vocal cords and not to sing at all. I don't know how it happened. But, even after the doctors' advice, I didn't take rest and came to Jaipur with my team to perform in a mega show. Perhaps, destiny wanted us to meet again in Jaipur.

I don't know why so many things happened in my life. However, the most important thing is, you were always a part of my life. Perhaps we were not meant to be. I don't understand why destiny allows some people to meet when there's no way for them to be together.

I must thank you for accepting me as a friend again. Earlier, in college, I didn't value your friendship and affection for me. May be I was so lost in my dreams at that time. I made mistakes in college days, I admit. I gave you so much pain in life. I almost ruined your life and yet you cared for me. Your parents welcomed me, as if nothing had happened. This was a great thing for me. I couldn't have asked for anything better than those seven days spent with you here in Rajasthan, the quality time spent with your parents, and your staff. To accompany you in your interview in front of the national media was a wonderful and special moment for me. The best part was that despite so many challenges and obstacles in your life, you never quit. I salute you.

I asked you to stay back with me last night in your study room. I had no right to. I just felt greedy and selfish. I wanted more of your caring, while I didn't give you anything in return, except pain, throughout life. I know and understand what I mean to you.

Now, I don't want to disturb you in your career. I realized my presence caused you distraction from your writing work. I don't want you to lose your writing momentum at this crucial juncture of your life. I want you to live the life of your dreams for your entire life. Hence, I decided to go. Singing is my passion, I love it. I wouldn't' leave singing till my last breath. My damaged vocal cord had caused me severe health problems. I think, my disease may prove to be fatal to me and I may lose my life in the near future. I am scared. You know, I have got a chance of a lifetime in the coming days; I am to sing in a most awaited event of the nation. So, with distorted throat and with even my life at stake, I will sing. If something happens to me, my life, I don't care. I am honoured to have received such a precious offer to sing in such a mega event. I can't miss that. But trust me, you have something meaningful going on in your life. Your family is beautiful. I am sure that in future, you will be able to write even better and produce blockbuster novels. If that happens, I don't want to be here, diverting your attention, because of my illness. The wrong girl will distract you; the right girl will motivate you.

I have seen your love. I don't want to see your pity. I am a singing star. That is how I want to stay in your mind forever. You know what? Till my last day, wherever I live, I will think of you. I thought of how hard it was going to be to leave you. But leaving you, yes, that is difficult. You are such a good-looking and caring guy, you'll find a lovely girl. I'll be a burden on you and your life. You need someone who will love you like you deserve to be loved. I can't wait for tomorrow. I hope you will take the literary world by storm in the near future.

I want to end this letter by saying something I wanted to say to you and only you, in this lifetime. So, here I admit. I love you, Keshav. I absolutely, completely love you from my heart and soul. And will do so till my last day, wherever I live. I promise you again, no one will ever take your place in my heart and soul. I love you not because of anything you have, but because of something that I feel when I'm with you. By choosing you, I chose happiness for life. You are the best thing to have happened to me. Beyond you, there is nothing I can see, love you dear!!

To love you is to realize that love happens only once in a lifetime and that life without you would be no life at all. To love you is to know that life is beautiful and worth living. To love you is to feel so special.

Sometimes the love of your life comes after the mistake of your life. That is what has happened to me. Goodbye, Keshav, Take care!!

Aditi.

I felt very weak, and my heart sank. The letter slipped from my hands. I picked it up and read it again and again, many times. Memories of our last meeting in college flashed through my mind. She had disappeared again. I called her number again. This time, it was switched off. I went numb. Nothing mattered to me; the guests at home, my interview on National Media, nothing. Aditi was suffering from a life-threatening throat disease, and she hadn't even mentioned it. How could she do this to me?

"Keshav beta, where are you?" I heard the voice of my father knocking at the door of my room. I couldn't move, kept sitting.

After a few seconds, mom and dad came inside. They were dumbstruck. My mom rushed towards me and held my face.

"What happened?" Mom asked, totally nervous and worried.

I couldn't utter a single word. My father took the letter from me and started to read loudly so that mom may know.

After reading the complete letter, my parents were numb. They couldn't find the words to console me.

Papa moved forward and kept his hand on my shoulder, "Beta, I think you should not worry at all. Of course, she has left you, this is so sad. But, there is something positive in this letter. I think you have missed that."

I saw towards papa with a grim face.

"Yes, my son, it's disheartening that she is suffering from a life-threatening disease and she has once again left you. But, at the same time, she has admitted and confessed the importance of having you in her life. Even she can't forget you in her lifetime. She has also admitted that you are the only and last person in her life whom she loves from her heart and soul."

Papa's words woke up my mind and heart. He was absolutely right. In the letter, Aditi had admitted that she loved me, a confession which I had been waiting to hear from her for so long.

I stood up. My mom hugged me.

"What should I do now?" I asked Papa.

"She has already admitted that she loves you, and then the only thing you should do now, is to look for her, somehow," Papa advised.

"She would go home first, obviously. Go to Delhi; her home and ask her parents. If she is not there, then go to Mumbai. Once you find her, with the help of her parents, get her admitted in a super speciality hospital for throat surgery. After she recovers, we'll talk to her parents for both of you," Papa continued further.

I was convinced now.

"Delhi, go to Delhi," I told myself.

I ran downstairs to the living room.

"Hello, sir. I am from *Dainik Bhaskar*. We would like to profile you for our Sunday magazine," a reporter said.

"It's an emergency, some other time, please."

"Okay, sir, on problem," the reporter said.

I asked Arvind to book a flight to Delhi.

33

Aditi's confession

April 2017

"I love you," the letter said at the end. I had read that line over a hundred times on my way to Delhi.

"Not fair, Aditi," I said to myself, "Not fair."

"I'll find you," I said to myself in a calm but decisive voice.

I reached Delhi around 10 in the night.

Next day, I went to meet Aditi's parents. They were stunned to know about the story I told them.

"Aunty, are you in touch with her since yesterday?" I asked her mother.

"No, I talked to her yesterday morning, when she was at your house. I contacted her in the night, but her mobile was switched off. And it is still switch off," her mother said, worried.

"But, beta, we were thinking that she was at your place," her father said.

"Uncle, she left without informing anyone."

"Where would be my daughter? What would have happened to her?" Aditi's mother cried.

"Don't worry Mom. Aditi is a mature girl. We'll find her," Gaurav said.

"Uncle, were you aware of her disease?" I asked.

"No, she didn't tell us anything about this," Uncle said.

"Aditi is lucky to have you who love her so much," Aditi's mother said with tears in her eyes.

"I want to show you something," she said and went upstairs to Aditi's room.

She returned within five minutes with Aditi's laptop. "Aditi has written a few pages about you in her laptop. I came to know and read all that yesterday only, while searching for one of her old music recordings," Aunty said.

I took the laptop, sat down on the sofa and opened the file.

Today, it's February 17, 2015; the cultural day in DTU. I'm writing my heart out here, as I'm sad toady, because I have misbehaved with my true friend. Today, I performed for the last time in front of DTU audience. I dropped out of B. Tech. I'm leaving Delhi tomorrow and going to Mumbai to start a new chapter of my life; to live a life of dreams for me; going to be singing star in Mumbai. Lastly, my parents have understood my feelings for music and now, they are not forcing me to complete engineering. I am grateful to my parents, especially my dad.

My life in DTU wouldn't be complete without talking about Keshav. He is a true friend. I appreciate his genuine caring and affectionate feelings toward me. I met Keshav for the first time in the second year of college. His honesty, his simplicity; his studious nature touched my heart and soul. He was one of a kind. I had ever seen such a guy. I knew, like other boys, he too had a crush on me. But, what I liked the most was his shy nature and respect for girls. These were the things which made me bond with him subsequently. Later on our friendship grew stronger when

I came to know that he was a devotee of Lord Narayana like me, had a dream of becoming an author. One more thing which was common between us was that engineering was not our first choice; both of us had some other dreams in life. So, in Keshav, I found a true companion who was having similar kind of life goals as I had.

Because of similar nature, he soon made a special place in my heart. I also used to motivate him for his study and life goals.

I became very emotional, when on my birthday, he presented flowers and chocolates to me. Any other guy, on this occasion, would have presented some costly gifts to me.

Soon, I realized infatuation and love for me in his eyes. That could be harmful for his career and he could have been swept away with that. So, whenever he tried to express his feelings before me, I would become too strict to him to make him focus on his studies and life dreams. When one day in a restaurant, he proposed to me, I was very sad. I didn't want him to indulge in love and any kind of relationship with me. I was his true and only well-wisher in the entire DTU. I couldn't see him go that way. So, I scolded him so hard that day, even I couldn't sleep properly that night. I too had developed a special kind of affection for him in my heart. But, I couldn't accept his proposal and see him forget his dreams. At the same time, I didn't want to be so harsh to him.

So, I decided to devise another way. I used to spend more time with him in college so that he may feel content and at the same time I may keep motivating him. Whenever he topped B. Tech, I would feel that as if I had topped, I was so much associated with him. In addition, to make him spend more time with me, I often invited him to my house. I would go to the temple, coffee shops, restaurants, etc., with him. He too started to visit my house very often and earned regards of my parents and brother. He would happily accompany me and took every pain for me during those journeys to live shows. Such an innocent companion is hard to find in modern days. I often would sing his favourite songs for him.

So, everything was going fine. But a sad incident happened in the final year itself. It was a fight among two groups of students due to our friendship. That day, I felt so humiliated. I knew that Keshav was also responsible for this to some extent, to popularize our friendship as a relationship among his hostel friends.

So, in deep grief and sorrow, I decided to dissociate myself from Keshav. I tried to avoid him, I disconnected from him in every respect. My parents advised me not to cut off from Keshav. In fact, according to me and my parents, this had happened because so many students were jealous of our friendship. But, I didn't pay attention to them. According to me, it was a slap for my self-respect.

It wasn't that I became hostile to him. I still had so many feelings for him, I still wanted him to achieve his goals, but I wanted to teach him the importance of our relation. So, I totally cut off from him.

Meanwhile, I won the music competition and got an offer from Geetmala, Mumbai. It was really an 'offer of life' for me. I convinced my parents to allow me to go there and fulfill my dreams. So, after a lot of deliberations, I decided to drop out from B.Tech.

When Keshav came to know about this information, he was restless.

On February 17, 2015, on cultural day, I found him waiting for me outside the green room. I felt sad for him, but remained firm. It was necessary to detach him from me, to make him learn to live without me, to achieve his life goals without my motivation. So, I left him like I had no relation with him. I was sure that it would be disheartening for him, but I did this for both of us. My parents asked me not to behave like this with Keshav, but I ignored their wisdom.

Today, on 28 April 2017 when I have come home in Delhi from Udaipur, to see my sick mother, I'm writing my heart out here again, continuing from where I left.

I reached Mumbai and with a lot of struggle, I achieved my dreams of becoming a playback singer in Hindi movies. I also launched a band in Mumbai and still go to various cities with my team to organize big live shows. I missed Keshav, in Mumbai. A true friend, like him, it's so hard to find nowadays. I missed him every day. Distance sometimes tells you the real meaning of closeness. A friend who understands your tears is much more valuable than a lot of friends who only know your smile. But, at the same time, I was satisfied that he would have moved on in his life after completing his B. Tech from DTU.

I was extremely glad, when during one of my trips, I randomly saw the novel written by Keshav in one of the book stalls. Back home, when I searched about him on internet, I found that he had become a bestselling author by now. I read all his books, all the articles in newspapers and magazines. At one time, I thought of contacting him and congratulating him. But, a voice inside me stopped me from doing that. How would I talk to him? What would I say? I had misbehaved with him. I had lost the right to talk to him when he had become a star, a successful author. So, I restrained myself from contacting him, for now, but would always keep track of all his success stories.

I often said to myself, "Dear best friend, I don't know why we stopped talking, but sometimes I miss you badly and your favourite songs are still on my playlist."

However, my destiny had written something else in my life. I got an offer to organize a big live show in front of thousands of audience in Jaipur. I went to Jaipur to perform along with my team and destiny again made me meet Keshav. But, I cursed myself when I came to know that due to me, Keshav had to drop out of his B. Tech, he had undergone stress, anxiety and depression, and at one point, even tried to end his life. However, at the same time, I was satisfied that he had become what he wanted, what he had dreamt of. At least today, I am satisfied in my heart that due to my efforts, my true friend had realized his life goals.

Anyway, when I met him in Jaipur, I found him still down to earth and having the same feelings for me. I realized what kind of place I had in his heart. He didn't associate with any other girl during his struggle and even in his success. I realized that I still mattered to him. I will have to return to him to Udaipur again to celebrate his success. I really love him. He is as unique as me. Unknowingly, I love him from the first day I met him. I always hid my feelings because I didn't want to shatter our dreams. At least, today, I am a happy and content that in our case, love didn't work as distraction; rather love has become an inspiration for both of us to achieve our life goals.

Really, I admit: the day I met you Keshav, my life changed. The way you made me feel is hard to explain. You made me smile in a special kind of way; you made me fall deeper in love every day.

Aditi

I was lost in thoughts after reading that confession from Aditi. All that Aditi was doing was for my benefit, to make my career, to make me learn to move ahead in life and achieve my dreams. Aditi loved me so much from day one, but I didn't understand anything. She was harsh, scolded me every time, yet she was always so caring. When I proposed to her, she became angry, rejected my proposal, taught me a lesson and didn't even talk to me. I didn't even understand her hidden care and love for me.

I started to curse myself. I was a bestselling author who was efficient to write twisted stories of love and romance, but Aditi… I couldn't even guess and think of her hidden affection, care and love for me. I was standing numb with tears in my eyes. I was speechless. I was regretting letting her go.

"Where would she be?" Aditi's mom's words cut through my thoughts.

Aditi's parents and brother became emotional to see my tears. Gaurav consoled me. Mr Kohli put his hand on my shoulders and said, "Come on, Keshav, you are a brave guy. Control yourself! Today, Indian youth looks towards you for inspiration, be brave."

I wiped off my tears, and tried to control my feelings.

"We have checked with all our relatives, but couldn't locate Aditi," said Gaurav.

"Keshav, Aditi likes you so much and she is fighting with a life-threatening disease. Now, all of us should put all the efforts to find her," aunty said.

"Yes, aunty, that's why I have come here."

"But, where would she be now?" her father asked.

"Nobody seems to know where she is," Gaurav said.

"Dad, Aditi has written in her letter that she will be performing on a national level event before taking any treatment," Gaurav said.

"But, the question is where that event will be organized and when," said Aditi's father.

"Uncle, I think it should be in Mumbai since she has been in Mumbai till now," I replied.

"Okay, then, let's go to Mumbai and find her," Aditi's father said.

"Not all of us. I think me and Keshav are enough. So, both of us should go," Gaurav said.

"Okay, then both of you go to Mumbai immediately. And keep in touch with every detail," Aditi's father said.

"Don't' worry uncle, we will find her," I assured her parents.

34

Searching for the love of my life

So, Gaurav and I rushed to Mumbai.

First, both of us went to Geetmala to get some information about her, but didn't get any clue. We then went to her rehearsal place in south Mumbai. We met her teammates. Except Aditi, every team member was present at that place.

The band manager, Abhishek, told us that after Jaipur event, all of them had returned to Mumbai. Aditi told them that she was going to Udaipur to attend a function. Since then, they were not in touch.

"Aditi told us that she had got some great offer to sing in a national level mega event. Do you know about that?" I asked Abhishek.

"She didn't discuss this with us. I think if that is a national level mega event, then she alone would have been invited to perform. It happens generally in those kinds of events. In such cases, event organizers arrange everything themselves, but call various popular singers to perform from outside," he clarified.

"Then, it will be difficult to locate her," Gaurav said.

"One more thing, I would like to mention," said Abhishek.

"What?"

"Since the last six months, Aditi had also started to sing in various live music shows independently," he said.

"Okay, what should we do now, according to you?" I asked Abhishek.

"You can search her in various live music venues in Mumbai as well."

"Okay, but Abhishek, you live in Mumbai. Do you know about any such event coming up, that would be so special?" I asked Abhishek.

"Right now, I don't know. But now, I'll also make efforts to find Aditi as she is our leader. If I find any information on the event you mention, I'm sure, I'll find it within a few days," Abhishek assured us.

We came back to the hotel, confused.

Now, Gaurav and I thought of going to live music studios or venues in Mumbai. We searched on the internet. However, I was surprised to see the search results. Thousands of such places popped up. In Udaipur, you would be lucky to find one place that played live music. However, here in Mumbai, there are an endless number of such places.

We felt small and insignificant. How could we visit so many live music venues in entire Mumbai? It didn't seem easy at all.

So, for the next three days, we went to a number of live music shows venues, but couldn't find any information about Aditi.

"Yes, we know Ms Aditi. But, she is not here right now," said the Executive Director of 'Western Live Music Shows'.

After a lot of search, we had come to the most famous 'Western Live Music Shows' to check about Aditi.

"Sir, how do you know her?" Gaurav ask the director.

"Last month, she sang in our music show. Aditi has great contribution in bringing our venue to the next level," he said.

"Okay, but where would be she now, any idea?" I asked.

The director thought for a few seconds. He shook his head. "Sorry, but, let me also try to find her. I'll let you know as soon as I get some information. Please leave your contact details."

It was our fifth day of searching for Aditi everywhere. But, we had not been able to find her.

The next day, I went out alone to search for Aditi as Gaurav was suffering from a mild fever. I wanted to stay up all day and look for Aditi in as many places as I could.

I was sitting alone in a restaurant taking lunch. Even at noon, on a weekday, the place was packed with so many people. Everyone around me in the restaurant seemed incredibly happy. They clinked glasses and laughed at jokes. Perhaps they didn't know how it felt to love someone for so many years, what was true love?

Although so many people had heard her name as a Bollywood playback singer, nobody had given any information about Aditi.

My phone rang, it cut through my thoughts. I checked, it was Abhishek; Aditi's band manager.

"Keshav sir, I have got some information for you."

"What?"

"Sir, today, there is a big political event at Brabourne Stadium in Mumbai."

"What's so important about it?" I asked.

"Sir, it's very important. Our Prime Minister, Shri Narendra Modi ji, is going to address a crowd of almost one lakh people this evening."

"How can it help us in locating Aditi?" I asked again, curious.

"Sir, I have got information, that just before the address of the prime minister, few prestigious and famous singers from all over

India are going to sing various cultural songs in front of the crowd. Just like it happened right before PM Modi's speech in Madison Square Garden in New York, addressing an Indo-American gathering in 2014," he said, excited.

"Oh my god! What's the occasion?"

"Sir, it's the completion of fifty years of Mumbai Cultural Festival."

"Right, but how do you know that Aditi will be there?" I asked, forgetting my lunch.

"Sir, I have confirmed this information through some of my friends."

"Okay, can I go there?"

"Sir, you need to have a pass for that."

"Okay, don't worry, I'll arrange for it."

Now, all links were interconnecting together. What could be more prestigious than this event, in which the prime minster himself was participating. That meant Aditi had written about this event in her letter.

Oh my god, I had seen numerous advertising posters for this event while searching for Aditi in Mumbai. But, I hadn't been able to connect the dots. Obviously, what else could be a better chance for Aditi than this? She was going to perform in an event of national coverage? I said to myself.

I came out of the restaurant in a hurry.

Using my reputation as an author, I managed a pass to enter the stadium within the next two hours.

Somehow, I entered the stadium, but still, I was so late.

Cultural folk songs had already started. India's leading singers were performing there.

The stadium was jam packed and I wasn't sure how I would find Aditi.

However, in the stadium, I found so many fans of mine. They recognized me. Fans were surrounding me from every direction for autographs in the stadium.

I was in a difficult situation.

I was in the crowd. My legs had given way by now; it was difficult to stand at one place. The crowd in front of me blocked me from seeing the main stage.

I elbowed my way through the hordes of people to get ahead, slowly.

Somehow, I reached closer to the main stage.

Meanwhile, I heard a female voice. '*Mera desh, mera chaman*'.

The bright and colourful spotlights from various directions were falling on the stage. It took a few seconds to spot the singer. It was her, yes it was Aditi!!

Aditi was singing with her eyes closed, completely engrossed in the song. She was singing a beautiful song. I said to myself, *Aditi, I found you*.

She held an acoustic guitar in her hand. A male pianist and other musicians accompanied her on the stage.

Now, I was suddenly excited. I was not tired at all. I was feeling more energetic. My heart was beating fast. My face was bright.

Aditi was singing from her heart and soul as she knew the importance of this performance. The crowd loved her performance and cheered a lot. She opened her eyes and smiled at the crowd's reaction. I was right in front of her; two metres away from the stage. She had not seen me yet. I waited for a few minutes for the song to be completed; I didn't want to disturb her in middle of the song.

As soon as I realized the song was about to finish, I walked slowly right up ahead to the stage and stood before her.

Her sweet voice vanished as soon as she saw me in front of her, right on the stage. The pianist and other musicians looked at both of us, surprised, wondering why and how I had reached there.

Aditi stood up straight. Her hands seemed to be shaky; the guitar looked unsteady in her hand. The pianist and other musicians announced the completion of song with an instrumental interlude. Aditi put her guitar aside slowly. I continued to look at her. Both of us stood before each other, silent and frozen. The huge crowd was confused at what was going on. They began to murmur, wondering what was happening on the main stage.

The prime minister had not arrived in the stadium.

Someone shouted from the crowd, "Aditi Kohli is a Bollywood singer, and another is famous author, Keshav Dixit."

"Do they love each other?" somebody asked in the crowd.

"Yes, it seems so..."

"Wow, what a love story!!" somebody said and the crowd erupted to see two lovers meeting with each other in a filmy style.

I didn't care for anybody. I just kept looking at her.

"Why did you do all this, Aditi?" I said slowly.

"I'm sorry," she said in a very slow voice.

A couple of tears came out of her eyes. I thought I would have so much to say to her when I finally met her. I would be angry at first; I would shout then, tell her how much she had put me through. I would then tell her what she meant to me. But, I couldn't. However, neither of us could speak; words seemed to refuse to come out. We just looked at each other and cried... and cried. I paused for a moment. I opened my arms. Amidst huge applause from the crowd, she moved toward me. I took her in my arms.

The crowd in the stadium again broke into cheers.

"I... I'm sorry... Keshav," she could barely speak.

"No, you don't have to be I'm sorry. I let you go. I didn't understand your true love and sacrifice for me," I was emotional.

She buried her face into my chest. We hugged each other hard and passionately. "Aditi, I... I love you from my heart. Please, never, ever leave me in this life. Thank you for coming back into my life."

She shook her head and cried, "I won't...I won't...".

"Now, I wouldn't let you go away."

She smiled and cried at the same time, wiping her tears.

We started to come down from the stage slowly.

The crowd went emotional to see both of us in tears, the eyes of so many were wet in the crowd.

The crowd began to make their way out as I continued to hold her and walk down the stage.

The security personnel escorted us out.

"Sorry, I left because I didn't want to disturb you..." she said.

"I am disturbed without you."

"But how did you find me...?" she said, still emotional.

"That's a long story, will tell you later. Why did you hide your illness from all of us?"

"I wanted to perform in this event."

"No, no more singing till you get treatment and recover."

"Okay, but where are we going?"

"Your home, Delhi."

I couldn't remember much of the journey except her beautiful face and the way it looked in the street lights. The city seemed more beautiful to me than any other night during the past ten days of my stay in Mumbai. I clasped her hand tightly, looking at her face. The reflection of the moon twinkled in her eyes.

35

Meant to be together

We were waiting outside the operation theater in Gurgaon. Both the families were present. We had brought Aditi to Medanta City in Gurgaon. We took the matter directly to the hospital management. We requested for a senior specialist.

A senior doctor suggested for immediate surgery.

As I was standing outside the operation theatre, I prayed to Lord Narayana. I was alive, but felt like my soul was on ventilator for the duration of Aditi's operation.

She remained inside the operation theatre for almost two hours.

Within seconds, the door opened and the senior doctor came out.

"The operation was successful; she will be shifted to the room in a couple of hours," he informed removing her gloves.

His words calmed my soul and I let out a soothing and a relaxing breath. I felt so relieved and thanked god. "God! You take away anything you want from me in my life, but just keep Aditi healthy, and both of us together," I murmured.

In the evening, Aditi was finally shifted to the hospital room. She was half-conscious as the anesthesia still had its effect on her. She lay straight on the patient's bed.

I went inside the room and sat next to her. I wiped my tears and kept looking at her.

She was discharged from the hospital after ten days.

She rested at her home and recovered completely within one month.

♋

So, after six years of friendship, struggle, drama, emotions and love, we got married.

Of course, both of us were very happy. It was a dream come true.

Aditi was blushing beside me. As a bride, she was shining as bright as a bulb that could burst with happiness any time. In India, marriage is the license for love. Both of us were full of joy and excitement.

Best feeling in the world is to marry your love with the parents' support.

Another best feeling in the world is being with someone who wants you as much as you want them.

If two hearts are meant to be together, no matter how long it takes, how far they go, how tough it seems, fate will bring them together to share their love forever.

True love never dies. It only gets stronger with time.

36

My happily ever after

And, there she was!

Aditi, my beautiful life companion!!

This was our first night.

That was a wonderful moment which I have re-lived again and again. We were together, just the two of us. That moment seemed to be a beautiful dream. The person with whom I was going to spend the rest of my life was right in front of me. I could look into her beautiful eyes, I could touch her, feel her. The delight of that moment had both of us spellbound.

This is her. She is mine now.

My eyes were wet. There was pain in them, but those tear drops poured a deep happiness into my heart and soul. My eyes were filled with tears of patience, love and dedication. That moment was untold, unpredictable and not less than a dream that had come true.

Words were unnecessary; the silence in the room persisted. And there we were, madly in love. Still not believing that finally, we had met each other. My consciousness asked me whether it was real and then it answered itself – I was not dreaming, she was real, she was with me. Deep inside my heart, I felt so satisfied.

We were lost in each other.

Gathering her courage, she looked up into my eyes.

"Aditi, I love you so much; more than anything else in the world. Please, never, ever leave me," I couldn't stop myself from expressing my feelings.

She just hugged me tightly and I took her in my arms. I could feel her presence in my veins.

"Aditi," I whispered in her ears, getting close to her, very close.

She was still breathing heavily and couldn't say anything. "This is a wonderful moment. I can't believe this. You are with me ..."

I further moved very close to her.

"Keshav," she said and grabbed my hand.

In a while, very slowly, she opened her eyes and looked at me and smiled. She was so happy, so delighted to have me so close to her. And she kept looking at me in that way, for some time. Raising her eyebrows slightly and still smiling, she asked me, "Tell me, how you are feeling at this instant, with me?"

I put my arms around her and I said, "Don't ask me. I won't be able to describe it. I just want to say one thing ..." Then, I whispered in her ear, "I am madly in love with you."

With that, I rested my chin on her shoulder.

"I love you too," she said and moved her fingers all the way from my forearms into the spaces between my fingers.

At that moment, I felt so complete. I realized how, just like me, she too wanted to live that moment as if it should never end. I held her in my arms for some time. I knew that holding your beloved in your arms that way is such a different feeling. But I never knew that it would be so magical. We were speechless again, just feeling each other. Silence was talking at its best. My arms were still around her, her hands were on my shoulders. I grabbed her and looked straight into her eyes.

"Love makes us really strong," I said in a trembling voice. "And it also makes us so weak. People in love can be so strong that they can take on the entire world. But then a strange weakness makes them so vulnerable."

She silenced me with a kiss. Her lips felt like warm honey. She kissed me for a long time, holding my face in her hands. I placed my left hand on her cheek.

We embraced. We kissed. Our hands never stopped touching. Every moment felt special as we made love. I saw tears of happiness in her eyes.

"Are you okay?" I said.

She nodded.

She brought her face close to my ear to whisper. "Yes, I'm okay, I'm great," she said. "And you?"

"I'm also okay. Your presence is unbelievable for me," I said.

Her warmth filled every pore of my body. Her hands moved continuously in my hair. My senses could not get over that intoxicating smell of her sweat mixed with perfume, till the first rays of the sun seeped in through the window to touch our faces. Her face was red and so was mine. That night, both of us completely forgot where we were on this planet earth.

That morning, my feet were a foot above the ground. This was the best feeling of my entire life. I couldn't have asked for more. My love was in my arms throughout the night yesterday. It wasn't just the physical acceptance that was making me feel that way, but it was the feeling of loving someone and getting loved back which was out of this world. It was the feeling of belongingness that was special.

37

Epilogue

So, it has been six months into our marriage and we are so much in love. It feels like every day we are falling in love more and more.

Fall in love with someone who wants you, who waits for you. Who understands you even in the madness. Someone who helps you, and guides you. Someone who is your support, your hope.

If you really love that person, learn to wait. Maybe you are not meant to be together today, but meant to be in the future.

Aditi and I, along with my parents, had shifted to Mumbai from Udaipur as Aditi had her work in Mumbai. We had bought a big mansion in Malabar Hill, Mumbai. When at home, we still talked so much to each other.

My fifth book had been released and also become a bestseller within three months of its release.

Aditi had started to get some big offers in Bollywood Hindi films as a playback singer after that event.

Both of us had become stars in our respective fields.

Both of us had faced some real struggle in life, and even couldn't complete B.Tech. Both of us were technically just dropouts.

Even then, we had achieved our dreams. We lived with our passion. So, we kept on trying until our passion became our livelihood. Both of us created our own opportunities. We didn't wait for them to come to us.

Sometimes, it's very hard to move on with your passion, but once you move on, you'll realize it was the best decision you've ever made. Success is no accident. It is hard work, perseverance, learning, studying, sacrifice and most of all, love of what you are doing.

Don't stop chasing your dreams, because dreams do come true. A dream written down with a date becomes a goal, a goal broken down into steps becomes a plan, and a plan backed by action makes your dreams come true. Never give up on something you really want. It's difficult to wait, but worse to regret.

Never be ashamed of anything. Make decisions. Make mistakes. If you fall, at least you fell because you tried. No regrets. It's life.

One and half years into our marriage, we were blessed with our little princess: Anaya.

My mother handed me the most beautiful gift ever, my little princess. I couldn't guess whether she resembled me or Aditi. I thought she was cute and beautiful like her mother.

The little princess made my family even more alive, filled us with more love and happiness. My life is complete. My love and my life – my family – are *my happily ever after*.